ANNE HOLMAN

◆

THE
TREASURE
SEEKERS

Complete and Unabridged

LINFORD
Leicester

First published in Great Britain in 2010

First Linford Edition
published 2011

British Library CIP Data

Holman, Anne, *1934* –
  The treasure seekers. - -
  (Linford romance library)
  1. Single women- -England- -Bath- -Fiction.
  2. Missing persons- -Fiction. 3. Mexico,
  Gulf of- -Fiction. 4. Love stories
  5. Large type books.
  I. Title II. Series
  823.9′2–dc22

  ISBN 978–1–4448–0632–8

Published by
F. A. Thorpe (Publishing)
Anstey, Leicestershire

Set by Words & Graphics Ltd.
Anstey, Leicestershire
Printed and bound in Great Britain by
T. J. International Ltd., Padstow, Cornwall

This book is printed on acid-free paper

THE TREASURE SEEKERS

Not comfortable with the genteel life of a spinster in Bath, Frances longs to go and find her father, Professor Arthur Cannon, presumed missing whilst on a plant-hunting mission in Central America. To her mother's dismay Frances happily joins her aunt and uncle on an expedition to the Gulf of Mexico. On the way she meets the intriguing, but secretive, George Webster. Her adventures begin, but will she find her father — and can she also find love?

Books by Anne Holman
in the Linford Romance Library:

SAIL AWAY TO LOVE
HER HEART'S DESIRE
FLYING TO HEAVEN
FINDING LOVE
HIDDEN LOVE
SECRET LOVE
CAPTURED LOVE
THE LONGMAN GIRL
THE OWNER OF THORPE HALL
THE CAPTAIN'S MESSENGER
BELLE OF THE BALL
CASSIE'S FAVOUR
THE GOLDEN DOLLY
A NEW LIFE FOR ROSEMARY
VERA'S VICTORY
FOLLIES HOTEL
VERA'S VALOUR

1

'Frances, what am I to do with my daughter?' The plaintive cry came from the young lady's elegantly dressed mama, Mrs Caroline Cannon, as she sat in the drawing-room of her gracious Bath residence in the company of her sister-in-law Mrs Gina Waybridge.

Seeing no show of concern on Gina's face, Caroline went on, 'Frances has always been such a strong-headed girl — and after hearing her father is missing in a Mexican jungle, she is determined to go and search for him!'

Gina said nothing and Caroline's voice rose high. 'Have you ever heard anything so ridiculous?' Having made clear her dismay, Frances's mama fanned her face vigorously as she leaned back on the pink-striped sofa bed.

Her sister-in-law, seated on a gilded chair, tapped her fingers on the arm rest as she replied, 'There is no need to distress yourself, Caroline. Though I understand you must be concerned about her adventurous spirit.'

'Oh, my dear, I am.' Caroline was grateful for some sympathy.

Gina looked down to hide her slight smile. Then she looked up brightly at Caroline's troubled expression, and said, 'But if you seek my opinion, I think it is most noble of Frances to wish to find her papa. What an exciting expedition it would be for her!'

'Exciting?' Caroline echoed, wide-eyed, sitting up. 'Ladies do not go travelling in jungles! Besides, what use will Frances be if she finds her father captured by native tribesmen?'

Gina pressed her lips together. After a moment she answered, 'If that is the case, and your husband is in grave difficulties, I agree, Frances will be able to do nothing.' Gina then shrugged. 'But we do not know until we get there. We may find Arthur quite safe, collecting his botanical specimens.'

Caroline leaned forward. 'Did I hear you say *we*?'

'Indeed. Arthur is my brother, as well as your husband and Frances's father. I, too, am curious to know what he is doing. The mail from Mexico is not always reliable.'

Before Mrs Cannon could speak, Gina went on, 'So, I have been thinking of going to Mexico myself, to make enquiries for his welfare. I should enjoy a sail across the Atlantic. I am certain William would love to go, too.' She paused. 'And with your permission, we could take our niece with us.'

Incredulity filled Caroline's face. 'I expect you to dissuade my daughter from her fanciful ideas — not encourage them!'

Gina smiled kindly. 'I know you do, Caroline dear. But the fact is, Frances is a grown woman. She is artistically gifted, and studious about the work she does for her father. And she is very fond of him. It seems natural to me for her to want to find him.'

Caroline looked lost for words, so Gina went on, 'William and I think Arthur has been gone far too long. Do you recall how long he said he would be on this expedition?'

After a pause Caroline cried, 'Heavens — he's been gone for three years! Not three months as he told me. Hand me my smelling salts, please.'

Gina handed the bottle to her timid sister-in-law, wondering what she could she say to comfort the poor lady of so little backbone. Sighing and swishing her hooped skirt, she stood and crossed the polished oak floor to gaze out of the long bay window at the beautiful stone buildings of the city of Bath. Once a fashionable city with a vibrant social life, it was less so now. Rain dulled the view. Thinking of sunnier countries, she spoke carefully.

'I think your daughter has an adventurous nature like her father. Frances will never find a suitable husband here in Bath. It is far too staid for her. She will never settle down to

4

genteel domestic life until she has had chance to see a little of the world. Travel is educational, and she might find a gentleman more to her liking elsewhere; even in a jungle.'

'Gina! Did you say my daughter should look for a husband in a jungle?'

Gina could not stop herself from laughing. 'Caroline, I know like most mothers, you would like to see your daughter happily married. I am suggesting that because Frances is unlikely to find a suitable man here, she should go abroad. She may meet someone, given the chance to travel.'

It was no use Gina saying any more; she could see Mrs Caroline Cannon was having the vapours. 'Oh, dear me,' she cried as she inhaled her salts. 'You may be right, Gina.'

★ ★ ★

Twenty-six-year-old Frances Cannon was tall for a woman. That was part of her trouble in finding a husband. There

5

were few tall men in Bath, and those she had met and liked were already married. So Frances had decided she might as well be a spinster and pursue her own interests. She made little effort to flatter the opposite sex, nor pretend an interest she did not feel. The only men she enjoyed talking to were hardened soldiers and bronzed sailors who had travelled. Their stories of adventure fascinated her.

So while her dainty girlfriends tripped around a ballroom, Frances contrived to engage a seasoned colonel or elderly admiral in conversation, so that they would tell her a little about their time in far away countries. As she listened, her blue eyes riveted on them and her soft lips parted, showing her absorption in what they were telling her, she longed to be there herself.

Of course, Frances's obstinate nature and choice of older men to talk to did not go unnoticed by the critical matrons at the side of the ballroom, anxious to see their own darling daughters married. They considered that conversing with elderly gentlemen was not the best way to go about it. So they were kind enough to sympathise with Mrs Caroline Cannon for having such a difficult daughter to marry off.

'Miss Frances Cannon is an attractive young lady — though a trifle lanky,' one lady remarked to another behind her fan. 'She is inclined to be so *individual* though. It is a shame for sweet Caroline Cannon that she has an oddity for a daughter.'

Her companion nodded in agreement. 'Her father, Professor Arthur Cannon, is a renowned scholar. They say he went chasing butterflies in Guatemala, or some such place in Central America. He has not been heard of for some years. He has simply vanished, so I heard.'

Overhearing disparaging remarks about her father, Frances was able to ignore them. In fact, she secretly chuckled at most of them. For Frances had a keen sense of humour. She set her lips into a smile, showing she cared not what the mamas thought, and paid little attention to their inaccurate gossip. Chasing butterflies, indeed! Her father's passion was for orchids.

Fortunately, Frances was content to be considered different — daring, even. Although even her papa sometimes used to sigh and say, 'My beloved daughter can, sometimes, be a little too reckless.'

There was another reason Frances yearned to find her father. As she explained to her favourite aunt, Gina, during a brisk walk by the river Avon, 'I'm lost without my papa. He and I have worked together since I was a small child and I found I could make accurate flower sketches for him.'

'You are indeed a remarkably gifted flower painter.'

Frances blushed at the compliment. 'I have drawn all the specimens Papa has brought back from his travels. But I'd love to be able to see the American orchids in their natural surroundings.

To draw them in situ.'

Gina nodded. 'There is nothing better than seeing the wonders of the world for yourself. Reading of other countries and seeing pictures of God's magnificent universe is interesting. But actually travelling, experiencing life in a country, seeing the landscapes, the animals and in your case the flora — '

'Must be heavenly!' Frances finished the sentence for her aunt, a blissful look on her face. The ladies looked at each other, their smiles turning to laughter. They were two of a kind; both enjoyed adventure. The thought of voyages thrilled them.

But they knew Frances's mama did not.

'So, how can you persuade my mama to let me travel?'

'Well,' said Aunt Gina seriously, 'any expedition requires a great deal of preparation. It would be sheer madness to trot off to some foreign country without planning. And the blessing of one's family is another necessity. So I told Caroline that I think you have an adventurous spirit like your father, and should be allowed to come with us. I assured her we will take good care of you . . . and after much persuasion, she agreed to let you go.'

'Dear Aunt Gina!' Frances clapped her hands joyfully. 'Thank you.'

A few days later, Mrs Caroline Cannon's relatives and friends heard that Miss Frances Cannon was to set sail for Mexico with her aunt and uncle.

★　★　★

'Mama,' Frances said at breakfast, a few days before departing on the merchant sailing ship to Mexico. 'Please do not worry. Aunt Gina and Uncle William will look after me. I shall remember to wear my sun bonnet, and change my underclothes — '

'My dear child,' exclaimed her mama wearily. 'You and your Aunt Gina have quite worn me out with your persuasive arguments to let you go overseas. I have said you may go with them, but I do not like it. I really cannot understand you. I wish I had a biddable daughter, not such a bold one. I just pray I do not lose you too.'

'I do not intend to get lost!' exclaimed Frances. 'I am only sailing to Mexico to look for Papa. I am not embarking for the moon.'

'You might as well be. You have no idea what you are letting yourself in for. You have never been abroad — '

'That is true, Mama. But Aunt Gina is a well-travelled lady and has explained to me that life abroad can be most uncomfortable at times — so I do not expect the trip to be as easy as a shopping jaunt. She has given me a list of what I will need to take. I have just helped the sewing maid to finish two light travelling costumes, and a durable riding habit. I have a trunk well stocked with stays, petticoats, stockings and drawers. Hats will protect my complexion from the sun, and I have bought a sturdy parasol — '

'You are more likely to need a gun more than a parasol!'

Frances smiled at her mother. 'Colonel Washburton has kindly lent me his pistol, and shown me how to use it. He has been tiger shooting in India, and he says the lions in South America are called pumas. Then, as well as huge snakes, called boa constrictors, there are any amount of smaller animals that need to be avoided.'

Seeing her mama's distraught face, Frances rose and kissed her tenderly. 'Mama, I am so keen to go on this trip, I have been studying all the flora and fauna. I completely forgot you don't even like spiders!'

'Ohh! Frances, say nothing more about what might be found in jungles.'

To divert her mother's attention, Frances plunged into discussing more mundane matters. 'Now, whilst I am away, Mama, our maids have promised to take good care of you. Cook will prepare your favourite dishes, and your neighbours — particularly Mrs Rice

— will visit to take you shopping, to visit the library, and to play cards. Mr Rice will accompany you on your visits to the theatre. And you have your embroidery to finish.' Running out of breath, Frances took a gasp before continuing, 'You will find Papa and I will be back very soon. And Papa will have some interesting specimens with him, I am sure. New seeds for your garden, I expect! What fun that will be for you to see them grow.'

Frances was pleased to see her mama relax, and take an interest in the subject of her garden, of which she was very fond. Her husband, Arthur, had brought back many new seeds and plants that she delighted in seeing grow.

Frances went on, 'Papa told me of a Scotsman, a fine collector of plants: David Douglas. He spent many years travelling and collecting for the Horticultural Society in California and has a fir tree named after him — the Douglas Fir. Would it not be nice if Papa had some plant called after him?'

Unfortunately, Caroline Cannon was in no state to consider David Douglas's achievements. Tears began to trickle down her cheeks and Frances was disappointed that her desire to explore the world was the last thing her mother wanted her to do.

Frances was not about to let her mother's nerves stop her. 'There, there, Mama.' She putting her arms around her mother's drooped shoulders. 'Think of all the wonderful stories we shall tell you when we get home. And I shall have plenty of sketches and be able to paint you some more flowers.' Frances glanced at the walls of the dining room where her framed flower paintings hung. They and others in the drawing room were all much admired by visitors.

'Well,' Caroline said, pressing her lace-edged handkerchief to her eyes, 'Of course I must have patience. I long to have Arthur back. I wish you God-speed. And I hope your accounts of your travels are not too hair-raising. All

I want is to see you both home, safe and sound — as soon as possible.'

Frances returned to her chair and resumed eating her breakfast muffin. 'Naturally you do, Mama. As we will be just as pleased to see you after our expedition.' Yet the thought of returning to a dull gentlewoman's life in Bath did not appeal to Frances in the slightest.

2

Life on board the cargo ship, which sailed from Liverpool to the Gulf of Mexico, was exciting for Frances. She quickly got over her seasickness, and became used to being rocked by the Atlantic waves. Watching the hustle and bustle as the skilled sailors manipulated the canvases of the square-rigged, two-mast vessel, she was never bored. She felt invigorated by the salty sea spray on her face, and experienced with awe the spectacular golden sunrises and red sunsets over the vastness of the ocean. Bouts of tempestuous weather frightened her at first, but she soon accepted that seafaring — or any form of travel — would not always be plain sailing.

Aunt Gina, a doughty traveller, showed Frances how to live as comfortably as possible in their tiny cabin. Her aunt was delighted to find her niece taking the sea voyage in her stride.

In fact, everything about the voyage, including the people on board, interested Frances. The captain informed her that Britain was friendly with Mexico and the ship's cargo of manufactured goods would be exchanged for oil barrels on the ship's return, together with ores, and logs of rosewood and mahogany for furniture makers.

The two women chatted, often seated on deck chairs, wearing sun bonnets in the warm sunshine as they reached the calmer southern seas.

One day as they neared their destination, Frances remarked to her aunt, 'I cannot understand why you wanted us to bring such a variety of clothes. Surely, coming in wintertime, all we will need is winter clothing?'

Gina laughed. 'Oh, you are not going to find South America like England, my dear. The weather in Mexico varies according to where you are. Expect what you get. Most of the time I understand the weather is mild. But at times it can be humid, or blisteringly hot. The rain can pour down occasionally and it can be very cold in the mountains.'

Frances exclaimed in delight. 'A land of surprises.'

'Indeed. On journeys, you should expect many surprises. Be prepared for anything.'

Frances smiled, glad to be away from the rules and regulations of Society in England, and feeling ready for any eventualities. She asked, 'And where does Uncle William think Papa is to be found?'

'As you know Arthur's last letter came from Villahermosa. He wrote to say that he was about to set off south, towards Guatemala, looking for new specimens of orchid and cacti. The jungle regions in the south of Mexico can be rainy — and very hot and humid.'

Gina thought it a good opportunity to remind Frances again about the difficulties she would face. 'We shall be plagued with mosquitoes and will need to use our hat and bed nets — and beware of the botfly — but we shall take sensible precautions to cover ourselves. And avoid provoking snakes or other animals which might bite.'

Frances nodded, taking in the information without becoming alarmed by it. 'I am looking forward to seeing all the wild animals — and especially drawing the exotic plants — but as you rightly say, as a novice explorer I shall need to be particularly careful.'

'Yes, you must always be sensible. But most of all you must enjoy your experiences, as I am sure you will. And we must find your father, too.'

Her scholarly Uncle William had brought with him a great deal of information about Mexico, and a rough map of the jungle area where her father was last thought to be. 'Much of the area is unmapped — ways through it known only to the local Indians,' he explained to Frances.

On several evenings William entertained the ladies by telling them more of what he knew. 'The Maya Indians lived in the area centuries ago. They were a marvellous people.' He went on to explain the little he knew about the ancient Mayan civilisation; the great pyramids they built, some now covered by dense jungle.

'Dense jungle?' exclaimed Frances. 'Dear me! Will we ever find Papa if he is lost in a tangle of trees and tropical plants?'

William smiled. 'I do not believe my brother-in-law has gone burrowing in tropical undergrowth. No, my dear, Arthur has more sense — and experience — than to get lost, and I shall tell you why. There is a wealth of magnificent botanical specimens to be gathered everywhere in the region. He does not need to wander far into unexplored territory to discover new plants.'

Frances sighed with relief to think her papa was safe.

William continued, 'He will have good native guides, too, I am sure. Also, he will have hired a train of mules to carry his supplies. If you ask why he has not corresponded with your mama for some time, I would think it is because he has been busy and time has slipped by without him noticing. Or he may have been ill . . . but, if so, we hope we will find him recovering.'

'Or could his correspondence have been lost?'

'That is possible. In wild areas where everything has to be transported by porters and mules, the Indians may not understand the importance of a bundle of letters.'

Travelling with them on the ship were a few other passengers. There was an elderly doctor and his Mexican wife, going to visit relatives in Mexico City. A balding businessman and a shoe sales-man, with names that amused Frances, Mr Clipperspite and Mr Pettyfoot, became friendly on the journey. They did not mind Frances joining them for an occasional chat. But one younger, good-looking gentleman, Mr George Webster — whose height even Frances had to look up to — was most dismissive if she tried to talk to him. Mr Webster spent most of his time in his cabin, or talking to his manservant, which she thought a pity, because the tall, lean man fascinated her.

He was, she guessed — and she had plenty of time to think about him — a man with not only good looks, but also well educated, and she considered him capable of doing many interesting things. Mr George Webster seemed to her to have an air of secrecy about him, too. He looked thoughtful; even forbidding at times. What made him so defensive? Why did he tend to look down his nose at her when she attempted to talk to him?

Curiosity getting the better of her one day, she asked him directly as she sat opposite him at dinner. 'Mr Webster, why are you travelling to Mexico?'

Mr Webster appeared jolted by the direct question, and slowly put down his knife and fork. His penetrative eyes made her recoil as he replied in a manner one might use to address a child, 'I intend to take photographs of ancient Mayan buildings and artifacts, Miss . . .'

'Cannon,' Frances informed him.

He resumed eating as though that were the end of their conversation.

'Photographs?' queried Frances, recovering her composure and looking directly into his eyes, making him swallow quickly and take a sip of wine.

'Yes,' he said, replying as if it were really none of her business but he was obliged to give some explanation. 'Photography is a new discovery. Light and chemistry enable images to be captured. However, I do not expect ladies to be interested in science.' He picked up his knife and fork again.

'Oh, but I am, Mr Webster,' Frances said enthusiastically. 'So please do tell us more.'

Mr Webster realised every passenger

at the long dining table was listening. Frowning, he continued, 'The photographic process is a recent invention. It enables us to copy nature exactly.' He went on to explain how photographs were made and began to reveal some enthusiasm for his hobby, which involved a great deal of heavy equipment. He had brought a brawny man, Stanley, along to assist him.

Mr Sam Stanley behaved correctly with the unobtrusive behaviour of a practised butler. However, he was just as evasive as his master if Frances questioned him. It was a pity, because Frances was keen to learn more about photography. It seemed to her to be wonderful to be able to make pictorial records of botanical specimens, because her father would find it most useful.

Both Mr Webster and Stanley appeared to wish to avoid her. Yet she persevered, endeavouring to learn more, questioning Mr Webster whenever she could, as it helped to pass the time on the long voyage.

'My father,' Frances informed him on one occasion when she managed to corner him, 'is a Professor of Botany. He collects specimens of flora for the Horticultural Society.'

He turned and smiled indulgently at her as he leant over the ships railings. 'Oh, does he indeed?'

Her heart leapt to see him smile a little. 'Yes,' she said, smiling back at him, 'and I make botanical drawings for him.'

'A very amusing pastime for a young lady.'

Frances, incensed, snapped back, 'I am a professional botanical illustrator, Mr Webster, just as you are a professional photographer.'

He stared down at the tumbling water as the ship cut through the water.

She went on, 'Papa collects seeds, and dries flowers by pressing them in between sheets of cartridge paper to take them back to England.'

'Is that so?'

Annoyed by his indifference, Frances

felt a desire to kick him. Instead she smiled at his stern expression and suggested, 'Mr Webster, you mentioned how 'shadowgraphs' were made by placing a plant on sensitised paper and exposing it to light. I should like to know exactly how you do it so I can show Papa.'

He then burst into such a bewildering scientific explanation about silver nitrate solutions, and silver chloride, of fixing the camera images of the photogenic drawings, that Frances' mind became lost in the flurry of information as she tried to grasp what he was describing.

'Gracious me!' she exclaimed. 'I find it difficult to understand.'

'Quite so, Miss Cannon. Now please allow me to get back to my work.'

She wished he was not so rude, because he seemed to have a wealth of knowledge. She had already formed the impression that she and Mr Webster could be more companionable, and she would learn a lot from him.

One day Frances was on deck and accidentally came across Mr Webster talking furtively to his man, Stanley.

'Have you checked the ammunition, Stanley?'

'I have, sir.'

'We must not be seen to carry any weapons.'

'I understand, sir.'

Frances blinked. She had not meant to eavesdrop. The pair were striding away along the deck, continuing their conversation, unaware she was there.

'Well!' she exclaimed to herself. 'I was not imagining it after all. Mr Webster is not going to Mexico merely in order to take a few photographs!'

Just what was he up to? Was Mr Webster hiding his real purpose for his visit? Could it be that he was going to shoot Mexican tigers? Or had he some criminal purpose in mind? She shuddered.

Should Uncle William and Aunt Gina be told? Frances thoughtfully shook her head. No, it was not their concern.

However, she decided to keep a close eye on Mr Webster and see if she could notice anything else.

George Webster was apparently a traveller with a mission — just as she was. He was often to be found reading, but it was difficult to discern what. It was not a novel, nor a tourist guide to Mexico. It appeared to be sheaves of paper. Was it some business he was engaged in? And if so, what?

Without staring at Mr Webster, Frances glanced at him frequently from under her lowered eyelids to observe his purposeful, easy-moving walk along the deck. She noted his long-tapered fingers tapping impatiently on the ship's railings, as if he were anxious to arrive in Mexico. His longish hair was dark, unlike her own, and whereas she had a neat centre parting and her locks combed neatly back, his hair was parted at the side and lay in wisps around his face.

And what strong features! She felt sure he had a strong character too.

Clearly he was a man who could use a rifle, and would manage admirably in a jungle, she thought with a grin. And she'd often heard him laugh heartily from afar when he'd been talking to his man, Stanley. So he was not without a sense of humour.

Mr George Webster definitely intrigued her — and Frances could not deny she was now attracted to him and she wondered if he was married.

As the ship approached the warmer climate it made Frances long to disembark. But as they approached the end of the voyage, her attention was given to her uncle, who had developed a nasty stomach illness, and both his wife and Frances were obliged to devote the last part of the voyage to nursing William.

3

Uncle William was feeling better, though by no means cured of his ailment, when they landed at the Port of Veracruz. With his wife and Frances to help him, he was able to disembark on his feet and direct the party towards a colonial-style hotel near the central plaza of the city.

Frances was delighted and amazed by all she experienced stepping ashore. Mexico's warm atmosphere washed over her like a silken sheet and heightened her senses. She was enchanted to see the natives' easy pace of life in the sunny climate, and the smiles on their brown faces.

'Just look at those colourful market stalls,' she remarked excitedly to her aunt as they rode in a carriage with their luggage towards the hotel. 'My goodness, there are pineapples, and melons, and grapes — and I have never seen some of those other fruits and vegetables. And look to your right — there's a grove of banana trees!'

Aunt Gina was less interested, being anxious to get her husband rested indoors. After they arrived, she was busy unpacking. Only after that did she begin making enquires to find out where her brother, Arthur, could be.

So while Gina nursed William, and they waited for news of Arthur, the days slipped by — until one day Frances could no longer resist slipping out of the hotel and taking a short stroll around. Her height, more than that of most Mexicans, gave her distinction, which made the natives regard her with polite curiosity.

The sight of the grand Spanish-style cathedral drew her towards it.

'Miss Cannon!' Her name was shouted like a shot from a gun.

Swinging around, Frances saw the lofty figure of Mr Webster striding towards her with a grim expression.

'My dear young lady, are you out of your mind walking out alone?'

Frances gasped at being caught, not tightly but firmly, on her gloved wrist by his strong hand. Of course she was well aware she was being a little rash. Going out by herself, she knew, even for a short walk, was never wise for a young lady — and here in a foreign country it was indeed madness. Nevertheless, there was no need for Mr Webster to be so unpleasant about it, she felt.

'My hotel is just over there,' Frances said calmly, pointing at the hotel whose roof was visible through some palm trees. 'I have only come a few steps, Mr Webster. I have been confined for so long, I need some exercise.'

By now he was very close to her and able to glare down into her eyes, which made Frances blink nervously. She had not felt afraid of being out amongst the friendly Mexicans — but she felt a little afraid of him.

'If you need exercise, then you

should walk around the hotel gardens.'

She was not going to allow him to tell her what she should do. She looked at him scornfully. 'I have already walked around the hotel gardens so many times, I feel like a circus horse. I need to get out of the ring.'

'But not into the lion's cage.'

She gave him a twisted smile. 'I really do not think it is any of your business, Mr Webster, what I do. At home in Bath I frequently take walks alone. I am not a young girl fresh out of the schoolroom.'

He took in a breath and blurted out, 'Miss Cannon. You are not in Bath.'

'I am well aware of that, sir!'

His well-formed mouth hardened. 'You know too little about Mexico — '

'Of course I do, Mr Webster. I have only just arrived. And I am looking around to learn more.'

He released her wrist and drew another long breath. 'Miss Cannon, before you learn more than you bargained for, I suggest I take you back to your hotel.'

'Why? I see no pumas ready to pounce, nor a boa restrictor hanging from a palm tree about to attack me.' She gave him a twinkly smile. 'Can you?'

'My, you are damned obstinate!'

'And you, sir, need to understand that some women are as keen to see the world as some men.'

He suddenly crossed his strong arms and began to chuckle. His expression changed from that of a schoolteacher's to become, so she thought, surprisingly attractive, as he shook his head slowly. 'Miss Cannon, you have a deal of pluck, I will say that.' Then he became serious again. 'I do not wish to frighten you. I am merely cautioning you. I do not suppose you speak any of the Mexican dialect, or Spanish, should you get lost?'

'How can I possibly get lost? You are like my mama. You both seem to think I intend to lose myself. For your information, I have a very good sense of direction. My uncle is still unwell and my aunt is occupied nursing him. When he is better, I shall have their company when going out. I should remind you that we came to Mexico to look for my father. And I shall never find him if I stay shut up in a hotel room.'

He loomed over her, as if considering what to say next. What he did say surprised her. 'Perhaps you would like a cup of coffee, Miss Cannon?'

Frances's face brightened. 'Indeed, sir, I would like that.'

He seemed to know where to go and soon they were seated at a café table with a small cup of delicious, fragrant coffee.

It was delightful for Frances to feel part of the vibrant, noisy, colourful life that was Mexico. Instead of simply being an observer — and being observed — at last she felt she fitted in, if only as a tourist.

She could sit back and look around at the Spanish colonial buildings at her ease; watch the stately, hip-swaggering figures of the native women, and the cheeky faces of small children as they stopped eating their slice of melon and turned to stare at her. She felt relaxed. She breathed in the warm air with pleasure, smelling the scent of some plant nearby — Mexico seemed full of beautiful, lush greenery. She enjoyed hearing the snatches of what was for her a foreign language, and basking in the glorious sunshine.

'Now tell me about your missing father, Miss Cannon.'

She was pleased Mr Webster was there with her, listening to her conversation as a friend might. Not only was he giving her his company, he was giving her a chance to enjoy being in Mexico. She studied him carefully as she might a new species of flower, and saw a different man. A more caring man; one who seemed interested in her.

Frances needed no prompting to talk. 'My papa is a well-respected horticulturist. He has a great passion for the cultivation of tropical orchids, and has been collecting specimens for years.

That is why he is here in South America.'

'Ah, yes. I understand orchids have become popular in England.'

Frances nodded. 'People build orchid houses to keep them at the right temperature. I draw them for my father, and the botanical drawings I make are printed as illustrations for his books. The longest description of each specimen does not appeal as much as a picture. A good illustration enables the reader to identify flora quickly. People also like to display attractive plant pictures on walls.'

'You must be a very skilled artist, Miss Cannon.'

Frances blushed, waving her hand as if to brush aside the compliment. 'It is what I do well. However, I do not suppose I am any more skilled at my flower painting than any person who is skilled at their job. Like you, and your photography, for example.' She paused, then looked at him quizzically. 'Or do you do anything else, Mr Webster? You strike me as a gentleman with interests beyond a new invention than making grey pictures.'

'Hmm.'

Mr Webster was willing to listen to her, but was evidently still not willing to tell her about what he did. So she went on, 'I am interested in seeing where orchids grow. They often grow on, or rely for support from, other plants. So I would very much like to draw them in their natural surroundings. Therefore you will understand, Mr Webster, why I need to venture into the jungle where they can be found. I am not a fragile lady.'

'Fragile?'

Frances nodded. 'Yes — my mama always claims to have fragile health. She could not possibly go traipsing though a jungle to find Papa. That is why I am here. I am young and healthy and, I hope, just as capable as any man of coping with the rigours of travel.'

He looked at her doubtfully and she detected some concern about her attitude. 'A lady would have to be fearless to face some of the tight places she might find herself in — especially in a jungle,' he muttered.

'There have been many female explorers. I cannot see that a woman would have anything more difficult to face than a man would have.'

He looked away and said almost dreamily, 'I would not want a lady to suffer hardship.'

He sounded sincere. She decided his hard shell had a much softer centre. Especially when a band of strolling musicians came by, and Mr Webster encouraged them to come over and sing to them — and then made sure they were well rewarded for their lively Mexican serenade.

But the minutes of musical pleasure were cast aside as the band moved on, and Frances resumed her opinions about the perils explorers could face.

'My Aunt Gina, Mrs Waybridge, has pointed out to me any journeys off the beaten track involve a certain amount of discomfort at times. One has to take the rough with the smooth. So I am not refusing to go anywhere for fear of what might happen. After all, I am not intending to go tiger hunting!'

He smiled, pursing his lips and leaning back in his chair to stare at the intense blue sky. 'You are very unlike most females who prefer an easy life, Miss Cannon.'

'So my mama says.'

'But, of course,' he continued, 'you are of age to do as you like and I can only advise you as a . . . friend. You ought to know that here in South America young ladies are carefully protected. If they are not, they are subjected to what is known as *machismo*. That means, a woman can be harassed by men. It is a game men play in this part of the world — it can be most unpleasant for a woman.'

She smiled. 'Sir, you may have observed I am exceedingly tall for a woman. I do not dress to attract men. In fact, men do not interest me.'

Suddenly, he laughed. 'I am quite safe, then?'

Frances regarded him thoughtfully, her cheeks becoming pink. 'From me, yes. But I dare say some ladies would find you very attractive.'

He laughed again as she blushed deeper, having admitted she found him good-looking. But amused by his good humour, she laughed with him.

'So,' Frances said, checking her merriment, 'you need not worry about me pursuing you, nor a plain Jane like me being pursued by Mexican men.'

He took his handkerchief out of his pocket and patted away the tears that had come from laughing so much.

'Oh dear me, Miss Cannon. You have an answer for everything, indeed you do. But as a man I will tell you that you are an attractive young lady — '

'You flatter me.'

'No. I am being honest. You are in no way protected because you think you are a blue stocking.'

Frances gave a little laugh. 'Dear me,

I said I was a flower painter — not an Oxford don. My education can only be described as adequate.'

'You are not a fool, either. You know perfectly well that you would not be wearing that enchanting cotton sprigged dress, nor a bonnet trimmed with ribbons and flowers — a hat any Gainsborough lady would be proud to wear — unless you wished to look charming.'

'Oh, do stop! I am modestly dressed in a gown suitable for a summer day. I can tell you that in Bath I am considered a very plain woman, and firmly on the shelf. And just because I chose to wear one of my best gowns for a stroll this afternoon — I go to work in more serviceable clothes. Just as you, sir, would not wear at work what you have on today — a smart frock coat with velvet collar and cuffs, slim-fitting trousers caught under the foot, and two-toned boots in the best of fashion.'

'You are very observant.'

'I am an artist. Trained to notice things.'

Mr Webster was chuckling. But his expression changed as he leaned forward over the table and spoke to her seriously again. 'Nevertheless, if you were my sister, Miss Cannon, I would tell you that no matter what you are wearing, you must not venture anywhere alone in Mexico. Even if you were as tall as a palm tree, you need a maid to accompany you everywhere here. In fact, you require an older Mexican maid, who is able to pour forth a stream of loud protests, and is capable of keeping men at bay. A robust lady's companion like that should not be hard to find. And if your aunt is not able to accompany you, then you should hire one.'

Frances looked at him thoughtfully, because she felt he was speaking the truth. But before she could think of anything to say, he continued, 'And I would make it clear to my sister that the jungle is no place for women. I would warn her against its many dangers — '

'Dangerous animals can be avoided,'

Frances interrupted promptly.

He was intensely serious. 'Ma'am, there are not only wild animals that lurk in a jungle. There are snakes and insects. Even the natives who live there can be injured, or bitten, by some.'

Frances found her heart beating faster as she admired the jewel-like brilliance of his eyes. He went on, 'There are rebels in the jungle too, Miss Cannon. Since Independence here in Mexico there have been many conflicts. Many warring parties fight each other; some hide in the jungle.'

Frances drained her coffee cup, thinking that he was probably right — but was he frightening her unnecessarily about travelling to find her papa?

'Whether or not rebels are in the jungle, they should not worry us,' she declared. 'I have no cause to quarrel with them. Nor they with me. I merely wish to find Papa and tell him that it is about time he came home.'

He gave an exasperated sigh. 'I see you are still determined to find him.'

'Naturally, Mr Webster. I have not come all this way simply to see banana trees!'

'No, indeed. I do not suppose you have. But your fanciful dreams of treading into dangerous territory are fine for a young lady reclining on her chaise longue in the safety of her home. The reality is somewhat different.'

'Mr Webster, I am no dreamer of dreams. No, indeed, my reading consists of the lives of many explorers, including a few female explorers. Women who dared, and continue to dare, to explore the wonderful world around them. My Aunt Gina is one of them. I only aim to seek for my father, and draw a few orchids in their natural habitat.'

He leaned back in his chair. He looked at her thoughtfully. 'Then I must speak to your aunt and uncle.'

Frances was unsure if he meant to be helpful or not. But being optimistic by nature, she smiled back and hoped he was going to offer her aunt and uncle some useful information.

Having paid for the coffee, George Webster rose and escorted Frances back to her hotel. It was pleasant to walk next to a man taller than herself.

She stopped outside the building. 'If you have time, sir, would you show me the cathedral before you return me to my hotel?'

He hesitated for a second or two, then offered her his arm. 'I would be delighted, Miss Cannon.'

Walking arm in arm with a gentleman was a new experience for Frances and she had to admit it was most enjoyable. Indeed she began to wonder if she was correct in her conviction that she had no interest in men of her age — they could be most agreeable.

His conversation showed he knew a great deal about Mexico — he was so interesting to listen to that Frances did not wish to interrupt him.

Afterwards, she realised that during their time together he had learned a good deal about her — and although she had enjoyed his company very much, she had learned nothing about what he was doing in Mexico.

Arriving back at the hotel, Mr Webster enquired and was told that Mr and Mrs Waybridge would be happy to meet him to discuss the disappearance of Professor Arthur Cannon. Frances, disappointed at not being invited to attend the meeting, pottered about her room aimlessly. She feared Mr Webster might persuade her aunt and uncle to prevent her from visiting a jungle — but she hoped her redoubtable Aunt Gina would be no more persuaded than she herself had been.

4

Frances was furious when Aunt Gina came into her room and told her that Mr Webster had told Uncle William that he would search for Professor Cannon himself. There was no need for them — or Frances — to do anything.

'How can he be so arrogant? To think he can find my papa any better than we could?'

'I believe,' Aunt Gina said, 'that a young gentleman who speaks Spanish fluently as Mr Webster does, may be able to find your father more easily.'

'But I wanted to go into the jungle!' Frances pouted like a child.

Aunt Gina sighed as she sat down beside her on the bed. Looking after her sick husband had been a strain on her, but her expression showed she sympathised with her niece too. 'My dear, I know your visit to Mexico has been disappointing for you so far. But you may still have the opportunity to go into the jungle after Mr Webster locates your papa. It takes a great deal of organising, finding good guides and mules for a trek in the jungle regions. So having someone to do it for us, especially as William is still unwell, seems a sensible plan to me. I think it is very kind of Mr Webster to offer.'

'And what am I supposed to do in the meantime? I would willingly help you to nurse my uncle but you have any number of maids here to assist you. Maybe you should get away from the sickbed for a while and go out?'

Aunt Gina put her arm around her niece and hugged her. 'No, my dear, I have the hotel gardens to wander in and I wish to be near William.'

Frances marvelled at the love that existed between her aunt and uncle and wished that she, too, could find and marry a man she could love for the rest of her life.

'So,' said Frances in an exasperated

voice, 'I must sit here and twiddle my thumbs because Mr Webster says I am not to go out alone.'

'You will be pleased to know Mr Webster is intending to ask an older Mexican couple he knows to escort you around.'

Frances looked surprised. 'Is he? But where could I go? I have been around the plaza almost every day it hasn't rained, and around the cathedral several times — and all the parks. I visited the shops and the markets. I have drawn and painted all the beautiful flowers I can find. So now all I am interested in is seeing the jungle — but George thinks women are weak creatures who should stay at home sewing.'

Aunt Gina smiled at Frances using Mr Webster's first name. 'I do not think he considers you a shrinking violet. I think he admires your spirit. But he is right to say you need protection wherever you go. And so now you shall have Maria and Justo to take you around. They are, he assures us, a very trustworthy Mexican couple, willing to show you their beautiful country.'

Frances was cheered to think that with escorts, she would perhaps be able to venture further afield. But she was not convinced George Webster would make finding her father a priority.

'I think Mr Webster is an adventurer,' she told her aunt. 'We do not know what he is doing here in Mexico.'

'He is taking photographs. People long to see pictures of wild places.'

'Yes, but is that all he is doing?'

Gina looked at her niece questioningly. 'Why do you say that?'

'Well, it strikes me he has been here before and knows the area. If he takes a few photographs of the place it won't amount to much.'

'Well, whatever he is doing need not concern you. As long as he finds Arthur for us, all will be well.'

But it did concern Frances. Perhaps it was because she had little else to do except to wonder what Mr Webster was doing in Mexico. And when she heard the following day that he had taken a carriage to Mexico City, it confirmed her suspicion that he had no intention of putting himself out to find her father — he might take several weeks before he even began to look.

But just as Frances began to complain that her father would never be found, a surprise message arrived at the hotel from her father, Professor Arthur Cannon to say they must not worry about him — he had collected some wonderful specimens. It stated where he was, camped not far from Villahermosa, and now, he wrote, he was packing up and was looking forward to meeting them at Veracruz in a few weeks' time.

When shown his letter, Frances was overjoyed to know her father was safe, and immediately she wrote to her mama with the good news. But a little later, she felt exasperated. She had weeks more to hang around doing nothing. Then she noted Papa had written that he had collected so many specimens he had not enough mules to carry them all back. It was a great disappointment to him to have to leave some of his collection behind.

Inspired to think of a plan to help her father, Frances decided to organise a relief mule train to enable her father to bring all his carefully gathered botanical specimens home. Naturally, she would not worry her aunt and sick uncle with her plan; she would simply say she wished to ride to Villahermosa, with her Mexican guides, to meet her father. She would not mention that she intended go a little further towards her father's camp with the mules he needed.

And George Webster could not object to her expedition because he would not know about it until he returned from Mexico City, and by then she would have completed the trip.

★   ★   ★

Frances found Maria and Justo charming. Their dark skin and shiny black hair showed their Indian descent. They were far from being peasants, yet they were not Mexican aristocrats either. Frances suspected they had a high regard for Mr Webster, and for his sake they were willing to look after her.

They behaved like fond grandparents towards Frances, and she appreciated them. Their English was not good, but as Frances was prepared to learn a little Spanish, they managed to understand each other adequately.

As her Uncle William suffered a relapse and Aunt Gina was occupied looking after him, Frances was insistent in getting permission to travel along the coast road toward the Yucatan peninsula to meet her papa.

'There are so many beautiful flowers I shall be able to draw,' explained Frances to her aunt, 'if I am able to go there.'

Gina, of course, questioned Justo and Maria about the proposed trip to make sure it was safe. And because she was feeling sorry for her niece — knowing Frances longed to see more of the country — she at last relented.

'I expect I will need to take William back to England to fully recover,' said Gina regretfully. 'His days for arduous travelling expeditions are over. But I know you are dying to see the country, and I understand how frustrating it is for you to be cooped up here.'

'That is true. You have had many wonderful trips in many countries,' Frances said. 'I have had none.'

'I know dear, that is why I am allowing you to go. But you must take heed of Justo and Maria. Do exactly what they tell you to do. Promise me.'

Frances nodded excitedly. 'Indeed I will. I've no intention of having an adventure — or getting into scrapes.'

'I should hope not!'

Frances asked her aunt's advice about the journey. She packed her travel bags with what she suggested, as well as her paints and drawing materials.

Justo told her where to hire the mules for the trip, but at first he did not understand why she wanted to take so many animals. 'No entiendo,' he kept saying, until Frances managed to explain that her father, who they would meet, needed the extra mules. Maria was delighted, as they could carry extra food and camping equipment.

Frances made sure her aunt did not see her leave with twelve donkeys in tow. But she felt elated to know she had their blessing for her trek, and set off in high spirits.

When the sun beat down Frances used her parasol. She was unused to riding, and found the mule she was riding uncooperative, so it was a battle of wills for her to keep it plodding along the coast path. It was only when they passed a village with a vegetable stall and she was able to purchase a big bunch of carrots to entice the animal along, that her mount became more amenable.

Maria and Justo thought it a great

joke to see the young lady having to bribe her mule, but it worked, and they commented with nods and smiles at her, and many *bravos*.

Ahora was a word Frances soon learned. It translated as 'now', but in Mexico it meant later — or, tomorrow would do. The Mexicans were not strict time-keepers, and she could not ascertain from them exactly how long it would be before they would arrive at Villahermosa.

Sensibly Frances did not worry, adopting the leisurely pace of her guides and allowing Justo to lead the way, while Maria organised the overnight stays in simple houses that took in guests and fed and watered the animals.

Able to enjoy looking around her on the leisurely journey, she allowed the warm atmosphere to beguile her as the days went by. Everywhere she saw beautiful plants, friendly barefoot children who ran along with the mule train, and occasionally the long sweep of golden beach alongside the blue

Atlantic. And in the distance, were the greens of the forestlands.

'It is heavenly. Just heavenly,' she murmured to herself, ignoring her wilful mount, the humid heat and her soreness from being unused to riding for hours on end. But she realised she was missing something important — a companion. Someone she could make comments to and enjoy a joke with. She wished Aunt Gina was with her to enjoy the experience.

5

They had just resumed their trek along the seemingly endless coastal path one morning when Frances heard what she thought might be thunder — but, turning, she saw a party of horsemen riding fast towards them.

As Frances had hoped, the mule drivers made sure the animals were all lined up at the side of the road so that the four riders could pass by without a disturbance. Only her mule was not cooperative. It bucked and scampered about as the riders thundered nearer.

Frances was suddenly jerked violently and she felt herself slipping off her bad-tempered mount onto the hard ground.

'Oh!' she shrieked. 'Ouch!' she cried again as she felt the blow of the fall shake her skeleton. Sitting dazed on the path, she rubbed her sore elbow, annoyed, aware that the riders had stopped and noisy shouting had begun.

Not understanding the Mexicans' loud volume of babble, Frances remained seated, waiting for the argument to die down. Whoever these horsemen were, they should have slowed down when they reached her mule train. They did not own the road. They would have seen her party. She would ask Justo to give them a telling-off.

Then she heard a horse's hooves dancing near her, and she shrank away, hoping she would not get trampled on.

'Miss Cannon!' She heard a man shouting above her head and lifted her chin to see George Webster, feet astride, flicking his riding whip in agitation. 'What on earth are you doing here?'

She felt immediately delighted. His tall, athletic build was distinctive compared with the squat Mexicans. His good looks were pleasantly familiar to see again, but she was irritated by his belligerent tone, and replied, 'At present I'm recovering from a fall — caused by your party's reckless riding, Mr Webster.'

'Me, reckless?' he echoed. 'I am lost for words. What can I say to a young lady who is determined to rush headlong into danger?'

'You need not say anything,' replied Frances attempting to stand and glad to grasp his strong hand, which gave her a thrill as he helped her up. The strength of him putting her on her feet again amazed her.

He smiled, but it was not altogether a friendly smile. 'What are you doing with all these mules? I needed some urgently for my equipment. And what am I told? 'An English woman has taken them all off to Villahermosa.' '

'First come, first served,' Frances muttered, patting dust off her gown.

He snorted. 'You had no right to take the entire mule population of Veracruz with you!'

'That sir, is my business. I am sorry if it constitutes a problem for you.'

He gave a long, pained sigh. 'Oh, indeed it is a problem — and you alas are yet another.'

'Only if you want to make me one, Mr Webster.'

He glowered down at her. Frances pretended not to notice. She turned to look for her mule, which was occupied munching some greenery by the side of the road. Walking over to it, she feared it would be reluctant to let her ride it again, and would buck and jump, amusing Mr Webster. But the wilful beast brayed happily when she drew a carrot out of her saddle-bag and offered it.

Gaining confidence, she called, 'Lift me up on my mule, will you please?'

She tensed as George came towards her because she knew he had not come just to assist her, and would have plenty more to say. Although, with no effort at all, he placed his hands around her slender waist and lifted her easily up onto the animal's back. It was a joy to feel his strength making her tall frame feel almost fairylike.

'I must take all the mules you are not using back to Veracruz,' he said in a firm voice she was not supposed to contradict, 'so that I can pick up the rest of my equipment.'

'No, indeed you will not!'

He gave a loud, exasperated sigh. 'Madam, you cannot want a dozen mules. I need them for my important work.'

'I need them.'

He swallowed as he held the donkey's bridle. 'Whatever for?'

Frances, sitting on her mule, was able to look down on him and had regained her confidence. 'Mr Webster. You will not tell me what you are doing here, so why should I tell you what I intend to do?'

She sensed immediately that he did not like her attitude, so she gave him a little smile and continued, 'However, as I am not as secretive as you are, I shall tell you that I have these extra mules to carry back all my father's botanical specimens he has been collecting over three years in the jungle. Papa wrote to say he would have to abandon the results of much of his years of labour finding the rare orchids if he does not have the means to transport them home.'

Seeing him at a loss to reply, she added, 'There, you see that is a good reason, is it not? Now why don't you be honest with me and tell me the reason you have for wanting the mules?'

'I am a photographer. As you know, I have loads of equipment to carry.'

Frances was about to say her need for the pack animals was greater than his, when Stanley, George's man came up to them. 'Mr Webster, the men do not think we'll have time to return to Veracruz and collect our equipment. We should press on.'

The two men walked away from her and conversed quietly together. Then George turned back and walked purposefully towards Frances. She found her heart racing.

'Miss Cannon,' he announced with a twinkle in his eye that warned her he was about to spring a surprise on her.

'As you have the mules, perhaps we could share them? I will escort you to your father's camp and then we will sort out the problem.'

'There was no problem until you came along!' she retorted.

George moved closer. 'Miss Cannon, I know you are obstinate, as well as a born optimist — and maybe there is a lot to be said of being blinkered against some of life's harsh realities. But you must be warned that danger is all around in Mexico — and especially in the jungle. Even the jungle insect bites are unpleasant, and can be fatal.'

'Of course, I am aware of that.'

He frowned. 'I presume your aunt and uncle have given their permission for your expedition, and I am pleased to see you have Maria and Justo with you, but are you sure you want to take the risk of any . . . *difficulties* that may arise? I suggest you allow me to find your father, and you turn back to Veracruz when we reach Villahermosa.'

'If you are going in the jungle to take

photographs and I am going to paint flowers, why should it be any more difficult for me?'

'Because you are a lady.'

Frances smiled. 'So I am — but not an entirely stupid woman. I shall cope, as you will.'

He gave another loud sigh. Looking over his shoulder at the men waiting for him, he said, 'The men over there are anxious for us to proceed. I must go on. But I cannot bring myself to leave you. Despite your insistence that you will be safe, I would be far happier if you travel with me.'

His charming smile melted her antagonism. 'Well,' she said, amazed at his offer and glad to have his companionship, 'I suppose if we are going the same way, we may as well travel together.'

Staggered to find he cared about her enough to alter his plans, and had offered to take her to her father's camp — and that he knew where it was — Frances was secretly overjoyed. It was not worth quarrelling about the mules. No doubt her father would be glad of a few extra, even if George took the rest for whatever purpose.

Frances found it pleasant, riding with him by her side. She had the companion she had been longing for. And a handsome one at that! She soon discovered he had so much knowledge of the jungle that he reminded her of a schoolmaster. Yet he could be amusing as well as informative.

To her astonishment they did not go straight to Villahermosa, but suddenly turned right, taking a dusty track leading into the hills — and into the seemingly impenetrable forest.

Frances' heart leaped. *I am going to get my wish and enter a jungle!*

There were tracks only the Indians knew, and everyone followed in line.

Progressively surrounded by the dense vegetation, which hemmed her in, Frances gasped. She found the smell of it so overpowering, it made her breathe more slowly. Her heart beat thumped as the mules plodded further into the jungle vegetation, and for a few moments Frances felt claustrophobic — afraid that she was being trapped.

It was terrifying to see the path becoming too narrow for her to turn her mule around and head out of the jungle. Her head swam as she realised she would not know how to find the track back out, as it closed in after them. Perspiration trickled down her face and back, and her hands became so wet she had difficulty gripping her mule's reins.

She had difficulty controlling her desire to cry: *let me out!* It was only her sense of shame to be feeling so afraid, and that her weakness would be known to the rest of the party — especially Mr George Webster — which prevented her from screaming in terror.

Then she reminded herself that it had been her wish to go in the jungle, to see the flora as it grew in the wild, and that her panic must be conquered. The rest of the party were in front and behind her, and all she had to do was to go with them. Soon the track narrowed further in the dense vegetation, so that only one rider could follow another. And either side of her trees rose to the sky, completely blotting out the light.

A sudden chilling cry from afar made her skin prickle. She cowered as the mule kicked. 'What's that frightful noise?'

'That was the cry of a howler monkey,' replied George Webster in a clear, calm voice. 'It is probably two miles away, but you will be hearing and seeing plenty of them.'

Having him nearby was a great comfort.

The strange cry came again. Frances overcame her initial fear and quipped, 'Now I am really in the soup, am I not!'

George, from his position in front of her, chuckled. 'You are far from being in the soup. I have two experienced Mexican guides with us who know the area as well as anyone — but we must always be on the alert for unexpected troubles.'

'What is an adventure without a little danger?'

'Adventures are not always fun, Miss Cannon.'

Because she had already had a taste of being afraid of the forest, she responded with feeling, 'Indeed — but adventures are great fun to tell everyone about later.'

George retorted, 'That is, if you live to tell the tale!'

Frances gave an involuntary shudder. 'I intend to go on many adventures. This is only my first.'

He laughed. 'So you are not scared of the jungle now?'

She felt he was not mocking her — he must have been aware of how panic-stricken she had felt a while back, knowing how frightened people could be who had not ventured into dense jungle before. He was, she decided, being kind enough not to make fun of her fears. He seemed to appreciate her not having fainted or made a scene like a silly girl.

After a long ride during which time Frances became accustomed to the atmosphere, she was glad when they stopped and camped by the side of a river. It was a large clearing where she saw a tribe of Indians lived. The Indian people — especially the children — were full of curiosity at seeing her. Their big brown eyes followed her, and she loved to watch them too.

Maria had no difficulty cooking for the extra men who had joined the party, and some of the Indian women were helpful after being given the small gifts George had brought with him.

Frances was glad of the opportunity to bathe in a waterfall the native women showed her. Then Maria insisted on her wearing a skirt and on combing and arranging France's hair. 'You must look pretty,' she kept saying as she fluffed out Frances's curls and wound her hair into a soft chignon, instead of the tightly drawn back style Frances used normally. 'Mr Webster likes pretty women.' She winked.

Frances retorted, 'At the moment he is more concerned with stealing some of our mules than how I dress myself.'

'No, no, no. Men always notice ladies — and you have beautiful golden hair,' the Mexican woman said, brushing it lovingly. Then Maria proceeded to show Frances how to dab perfume behind her ears, on her wrists, and on the hem of her skirt while an audience of Indian girls watched and giggled.

Frances was not naïve. She understood Maria was trying to tell her that she should flirt with George. But she was not seriously interested in men — or had she changed her mind? Just a little, perhaps.

George Webster was undoubtedly a good-looking man. His physique was admirable. His long straight legs were shown off well by jodhpurs, and his wide shoulders by a hunting jacket. Since she'd known him, his features had become more relaxed and his good humour more obvious. He was now being more affable, but that, she decided, was because he had worked out how he could make use of the mules she had. But being honest with herself, she could not deny George was more to her than just an interesting person. Frances had to admit she had become attracted to him.

Here she was, deep in a Mexican jungle, something she'd been longing to experience, and having supper in an Indian village. She knew she should be thinking of meeting her father, or of listening to the strange birds and animals noises she could hear. She should be planning to draw some of the exotic plants growing around when it became light in the morning — not concentrating on what she thought about George Webster and whatever he might be up to.

As she reflected, George came over holding a plate of beans and tortillas, the same as she had been given, and sat down cross-legged beside her.

'I hope you can manage to eat this Mexican food.'

Frances was having some difficulty in enjoying it, but said bravely, 'I dare say I shall get used to hot chillis.'

She could not expect European food in the jungle; she knew she had to adapt to everything when travelling. Just as she had put up with the oppressively hot sunshine while they had been riding that day, and would have a narrow, uncomfortable camp bed that night. Inconveniences she had been warned about, not only by George, but by Aunt Gina too.

But she was not prepared for the next shock.

6

Having eaten, George lay back, yawned, and closed his eyes as if he was prepared to sleep. But he opened one eye, and said casually, 'For your safety, we think it is best to tell the natives that you and I are man and wife.'

'What?' exclaimed Frances, her eyes bulging.

'You heard what I said. You have to understand I have to protect you from harassment — we have to have a good reason for you being with us. Or all the men will think you are fair game. Especially as you are looking very attractive tonight.'

Frances was momentarily lost for words, but not for long. 'I think you presume too much.'

'What you think does not matter. The decision has been made for your safety. And in the jungle you have to do what your guides advise, or you are in trouble.'

Frances could not at that moment think of any worse trouble than suddenly finding she was married to Mr George Webster!

You are joking, of course,' she said with a feeble laugh.

'No.' His face was calm.

Frances was dismayed. Her heart was pattering as she stumbled with the words. 'Then why must you say we are married? Why tell a lie?'

'People in these parts expect a woman of your age to be married.'

She flinched with embarrassment, knowing that was true even in England for women of her age. She retorted, red-faced, 'I am not what people consider an attractive female.'

He grinned. 'How many times do I have to tell you that you are? Do you think I would be bothering to guard you if you were not?'

She was half flattered, and half suspicious, and remained silent.

He cleared his throat. 'Tonight in the firelight you hair looks spun with gold, your whole body looks feminine and graceful in a dress, now you have taken off your military-style riding clothes — '

'Oh, do stop teasing me!'

'I am being quite honest with you. In fact I no longer think of you as a mere responsibility — I think of you like my sister, whom I have to protect.'

She detected his sincerity. 'Thank you,' she murmured. She had not meant to give him the burden of her presence. Their meeting had been accidental. But she felt in her heart that he was trying to be sensible — and she should not be ungrateful.

She tried to regain her composure. 'Mr Webster, how would the natives possibly know whether I was married or not?'

'They would notice if a young woman was sleeping alone,' he went on to explain. 'They would not understand why you came — unless you are here to serve your husband.'

She was alarmed. Surely George would not force her to . . . no, no. She must keep calm. She asked cautiously, 'And what exactly do you mean by saying I must pretend to serve you?'

He grinned. 'You must give the impression that you care about me, as a good wife should. Make sure I have enough food, clean clothes, et cetera.'

She did not like to pursue the et cetera but asked, 'And what are you expected to do?'

'I, as your husband, will show I care for you and protect you. And keep the other men at bay.'

His eyes were twinkling and she suspected he was enjoying teasing her. But there was truth in his argument that she needed a protector. In the environment she found herself in, especially, she felt very vulnerable. It struck her that she was heartily glad he was with her. And what harm would there be in pretending she was married to him? Yet she was loath to agree.

Sensing her reluctance, he became serious. 'You may find worse things happening to you before you come out of the jungle, Frances, than pretending to being married to me.'

She acknowledged that could be so.

He seemed to understand she was not overjoyed to find she had to accept a close relationship with him. He cleared his throat, and said, 'I have no intention of holding you to our pretend marriage when this expedition is over. I have only your safety in mind — at present.'

It seemed embarrassingly necessary. 'Oh dear, I see I should accept your suggestion,' she said stiffly — though inside she felt like soft cheese.

Without showing any pleasure at her agreement to their mock marriage, he wiped his hand over his face and said, 'I think we should go to bed now. We have endured a long ride, and we shall face another tomorrow.' He gave a long yawn. 'It is essential that we are alert when travelling. Come along, I shall show you our tent.'

Wide-eyed, Frances almost whispered, 'Do you mean that we must sleep in the same tent?'

'I do. But,' he added with another yawn, 'you will be unmolested, I assure you. Just as if you were sleeping in a tent of your own.'

'What about my reputation?'

He grinned. 'Lost in the jungle, I am afraid. But any lady that ventures abroad and into wild places risks being thought of as unconventional. You are an intelligent lady, Frances, and you must have known that when you embarked on this . . . *adventure*, as you like to call it, there were bound to have to be compromises at times. Is that not so?'

Frances was baffled to know how to reply.

George suddenly looked directly into her startled eyes. 'Before you think that you are being asked to do something against your principles, young lady, I have already told you, you will not be in any danger from me. I have thought about you a great deal since I met you on the road to Villahermosa. I consider you an attractive lady, even when you are sitting on the ground having fallen off your mule. You have neat ankles, and other agreeably shaped features, although you are tall for a lady — and as I have mentioned, that burnished golden hair of yours is truly magnificent in this evening's firelight. People here will understand why we are together if we are married. And, I think if we are willing to tolerate the situation with good humour, you can come out of this adventure without losing your expectation of a good marriage back in England.'

'Being married, all of a sudden, exceeds all my expectations!'

George chuckled. 'Don't forget I have to bear the inconvenience of being married to you!'

'You, inconvenienced?'

'Yes, indeed. I am a bachelor. And I intend to remain one. But if I ever decide to marry I would wish to choose a lady, not have one thrust on me.'

Hurt that he could seem suddenly so ungallant, after all the flattery, Frances cringed inside. It was true she could have retorted that he was not her choice either, but the truth was that she did feel attracted to him.

Pushing her plate away, Frances knew she would be hungry that night, but nothing could be as inconvenient as having to share a tent with a reluctant groom. What could she do about it?

Most probably no one would bother to notice her blushes. The Indians, she guessed from what George had said, had already been told that they were man and wife, and the rest of the party were amused by the arrangement. And, no doubt, Maria would tease her unmercifully.

Frances looked around at the dense green vegetation surrounding them. She had longed to be in the jungle; and now here she was. That evening the thickly forested hills seemed vast, mysterious, and frightening. The calls of the howler monkeys and great birds seemed eerie. The mosquitoes bit painfully if one's skin was not covered. She had no idea exactly where she was, nor how to get out of the jungle if she wanted to. She had allowed herself to be escorted here — and now must bear the consequences.

She realised it was wise to sleep near George — there was no point in being missish about it.

'Very well,' she said with a nervous grin. 'I only hope you do not snore.'

He leaned over and placed something small in her hand. Looking down at it, Frances saw it was a ring.

'I borrowed this from Maria. We thought it would fit your finger.'

Frances had no idea on which finger a wedding ring was supposed to go, never having discussed marriage prospects with girl friends. But George lifted her left hand and slid the ring onto her fourth finger, saying, 'There, Mrs Webster — a perfect fit. Now let us retire.'

She was indeed very tired. Going to bed down in his tent seemed unreal — but he left her to retire alone.

Snuggling down in her camp bed, Frances fortunately had no time to think about the peculiar situation she was in. She was comforted to believe George Webster was a man she could trust to keep to his word to treat her as a sister who needed looking after.

Later, when they were almost invisible to each other under their mosquito nets, they both slept almost as soon as they laid down their heads.

* * *

Frances awoke in the morning to hear a strange noise near her bed. Afraid, she looked quickly over towards George's bed to find it empty.

Shutting her eyes, thinking a few minutes' more sleep would be wonderful, she felt something cold touch her nose. Brushing it aside, she was aware that the soft dampness was pressing on her nose again.

A chattering noise made her open her eyes, wide — only to see a blackfaced monkey, which had pushed her mosquito net aside, offering her a banana by pressing it on her nose!

Struggling to keep her panic under control, she took the banana nervously. The animal then leapt onto her bed and began to jump up and down — and he was no lightweight!

This is breakfast in bed with a difference, she thought wryly, trying vainly to shoo her visitor away.

Sitting up, she suddenly became aware that several small laughing faces were peering into the tent, watching with delight as the monkey took some of her clothes in his long arms and draped them over himself as he pranced around, making monkey cries.

Frances was laughing too as Maria came to her rescue. 'Shoo! Away with you children! And take your pet monkey with you.'

The children called to the animal and quickly vanished, still giggling.

Maria turned to Frances and asked with a broad grin, 'And how was your wedding night, Mrs Webster?'

Frances was immediately reminded

of her embarrassing married state, and thought it best to be good-humoured. 'Fine, thank you,' she replied with a brave smile. 'I slept well.'

Maria was chuckling to herself as she collected the clothes strewn around the tent. 'Hurry. We go soon,' she said.

Frances was saddle-sore, she wanted to lie abed — but she was conscience-stricken. Maria was over twice her age, yet she had been cooking for the whole party and, with good humour, was ready to tackle another day's journey. Were Mexican women tougher than the English — or were they not as lazy as people said the Mexicans were?

Frances got out of bed and hurried to complete her toilet.

George was busy readying the mule train for moving on. He had, without consulting Frances, decided they could do without the Mexican drovers they had brought from Veracruz, and having paid them, sent them back. The four men who had joined the party with him, besides Maria, Frances and Justo, were now the only people going on further into the rainforest to find her father's camp.

Frances was not surprised to hear a few remarks made in fun about her new married state, nor to be called 'Mrs Webster.' It was all part of the charade she had to play. She hoped that, after a while, the teasing about their 'marriage' would stop.

★ ★ ★

They rode on through the thick tropical forest for several hours, sometimes pushing through dense jungle trails and sometimes meeting brooks and rivers and small clearings made by an Indian tribe. Lacy mists sometimes covered their way. Great care had to be taken not to get caught up in swampy lagoons or Indian traps.

She had little contact with George, who led the way with a guide. Still burning with curiosity to find out why he was being so reticent in telling her why he was in the jungle, after they stopped for a meal she decided to question Sam Stanley.

'We are looking for your father's camp,' Sam answered her stonily.

Frances retorted crossly, 'If you think you are fooling me into believing that is why you and Mr Webster came here, then think again.'

Sam looked at her warily as she went on, 'I know you men are here for a different reason than 'taking a few photographs', as I was told. It is too dark in the jungle. And even when we reach open areas, I find I have no time to open my sketchbook and draw the plants. Neither have you time to set up your equipment and go though the complicated process of photography.'

'If you want to know any more, you will have to ask Mr Webster, ma'am.'

As Frances had suspected, there was more to their journey. In frustration she cried, 'I have tried to find out from him, but he is close-lipped. But you can tell him from me that I am not fooled by all this criss-crossing along jungle paths. You are looking for something, I strongly believe.'

Frances had doubted if Sam Stanley could ever smile — but he did now, a slight smirk. 'I will inform him about your curiosity, Mrs Webster,' he said, giving her a slight bow.

Frances, unperturbed by his unfriend-liness, smiled back. 'And you may add that if he should tell me any secrets, I am hardly going to be able to gossip about them to my friends.'

She was attempting to joke, but she could see that Stanley was not receptive to humour. Nor, it seemed, did he approve of her presence. Anyhow, she now strongly suspected that George and Stanley were engaged in some serious business.

However, George was not able to discuss anything with her that night. He was deep in consultation with the other men and after finishing their discussion, he was exhausted. He collapsed onto his bed after the evening meal and was immediately in a deep sleep.

Frances, who had been helping Maria with the cooking and clearing up, had no choice but to retire to bed hearing George's deep breathing.

★ ★ ★

The following midday, after the party had dismounted in a small clearing by a brook to water the mules, and to take some refreshment, Frances knew there would be a little time for her to make a quick drawing. So she took her sketchbook and ventured a little way into the vegetation, seeing a beautiful orchid she wished to draw. But the best flowers were a little further away and she stepped towards them.

Then, suddenly, she felt the ground giving way.

She felt herself slipping . . . and falling . . . tumbling under the ground . . .

She screamed.

Landing on soft earth, Frances lay shocked after her fall. Gasping after being winded, she wondered where she was. She could see nothing, and was frightened to move much at first. After a while, her senses returned and she realised she was in great trouble. She had not mentioned to anyone that she was going to make a sketch. Tentatively, she tried to stand.

Then — whoops! She felt her feet giving way again: She was slipping further down and cried out as she fell, landing on a pile of vegetation.

Ouch! She had hurt her ankle. But worse, she was now in total darkness.

Fearful she was in a pit, and that no one would know where she was, she moaned in despair. She was trapped. Snakes, spiders, biting ants — all the creatures she had been instructed to avoid — came into her mind. Would she ever be found so deep underground?

Her daring spirit vanished. For the first time, Frances Cannon felt a real fear of being smothered by the Mexican rainforest — and wished she was safely home in Bath.

7

Hours must have passed. Occasionally Frances heard people shouting her name from afar. It was comforting to know they were looking for her and had not left the area. But they obviously could not hear her answering cries for help.

She had yelled back a hundred times, 'Help me! I've fallen into a deep hole.' Or was it a trap she was in, built by the Indians to catch wild animals? When would they come and release her?

She had hurt her ankle in the fall, and it ached.

As more time went by and her cries were not answered, Frances felt panic overtake her. Wild speculation seized her as she realised she would be left in this dark, dank tomb to rot — eaten alive by ants or snakes that lived on the jungle floor. Chilled now, and afraid to move, Frances sat shuddering in fear.

'Mrs Webster! Mrs Webster, are you there?' She was sure it was Justo she could hear calling.

He seemed not far away and she yelled back as loud as she could. But he did not answer. He obviously had not heard her. He must be traversing the area, not imagining that she may lie below the surface.

They still believed she must be in the area, thank God. She tried to cry louder when she heard another call but she was now becoming hoarse — her voice only a croak.

Trying again to stand, Frances realised she must have twisted her ankle as acute pain shot through her leg and made her sink down again in a hurry.

Complete misery then overtook her as the people calling her faded away. She felt sure she would die here in this great cavern of a pit in the jungle. Tears fell down her cheeks and she wept. She could blame nobody but herself. She had stepped away from the clearing

— only a few steps, that was true — and the jungle had swallowed her up.

How long she remained in this state of despair she never knew. She did not know if it was night or day. She might have dozed, because the earth was soft — though she hoped jungle beetles were not crawling over her.

Suddenly there was a rustling noise from above. She became aware of movement over her head. Some animal had found her — and was coming to attack her! Frances moaned in fear.

Suddenly there was a plop as if something heavy had fallen down beside her. She held her breath, wanting to scream but not daring. Was it a wild cat? Something was moving about coming nearer.

It was an animal that grunted, and she gave a terrified cry as it touched her hand. Furry fingers stroked her face as she drew away.

Then she recognised the woofs and grunts of a howler monkey. She jumped as it made the most frighteningly loud howl.

But the animal did not attack her. It sat down beside her and chattered, taking her hand and holding it.

'Oh dear!' she sobbed. 'How ironic that an animal should come, not to attack me, but to keep me company.'

The monkey left her to prance about the cavern, but always returned to sit by her, and to howl every so often.

Then, as quickly as it had come, it was gone.

It must have found some way to crawl out. And if the monkey could get away, then so could she.

On her hands and knees she moved tentatively around, feeling the edge of the pit, but she felt only hard rock. Left alone, Frances began to lose hope and to suffer mental death throes — until she heard the monkey return. Jumping down beside her, it lifted her hand and placed a banana in it!

Frances wept with relief. She was sure this monkey was the pet from the Indian village that had been brought to find her. So she must wait until the monkey's howling brought her rescuers to the place where she had fallen.

It seemed an impossible dream. Losing all sense of where she was — becoming unconscious at times — finally she heard her rescuers above calling to her. 'Mrs Webster, are you there?'

Frances croaked back. At last someone answered. Beams of light crossed over her. They had found her!

There was a scramble of feet and talking. 'Careful now, the ground may give way,' she heard among the many excited Mexican voices.

A strong light flashed over her. 'Stay where you are!' She heard George's firm voice from above.

'I can't move. I've hurt my foot.' She struggled to be heard.

A little later Frances was aware of more light around her, and closed her eyes. The relief of knowing she was being rescued was heightened by recognising it was George who was lifting her and carefully clasping her to his body before being hoisted out of the pit. She clung to him gratefully.

She learned later that a great deal of care was needed for them to bring her to the surface. A rope tied to a Banyan tree enabled George to be lowered into the hole and then he had to help the injured woman up out of the deep hole, which took time.

Back on the surface she felt overjoyed to be safe — yet humiliated to have been so much trouble to the party.

'I am sorry,' she kept murmuring, as Mr Webster trickled water over her face and lips, aware that he was not cross with her as he could very well have been. He carried her into their tent and gently laid her on her camp bed, where Maria fussed around her.

★　★　★

Frances recovered remarkably quickly after her ordeal. Everyone had been kind and not scolded her, although she scolded herself for her stupidity. After a rest, wash, sleep and some food, she would have been up on her feet again — only she had a very sore ankle.

'How long was I lost?' she asked Maria, who was washing her hair.

'Two days, Mrs Webster. Big worry for us.'

Frances apologised again for her carelessness, but Maria said, 'You not far away. It was, how do you say under . . . ?' Maria pointed to the ground.

'The forest floor,' said Frances. 'It gave way.'

'Yes, yes,' Maria said with a smile. 'The men are very pleased.'

Frances blinked. Why should the men be pleased she had fallen into a hole? Perhaps they resented having a woman travelling with them, and were glad to know she had got into trouble. Yet she did not feel the Mexicans resented her. They were good-natured, polite to her, and easily amused. But perhaps that was only because they respected George Webster — and thought she was his wife.

She noticed that the party seemed to have decided to stay a while in the area. There was no attempt to saddle up and load the mules ready to move off. Her escapade had stopped the party's progress. She felt guilty.

'George,' Frances called as he rushed into the tent to fetch his sun hat.

His face turned towards her. Such a handsome face he had, but it was his concern she appreciated as he asked, 'Are you all right?'

'Yes, thank you — only my ankle hurts.'

'Don't get up, then. I'll ask Maria to bring you some coffee.'

'I must apologise again for being so careless and causing everyone so much trouble.'

He turned to face her, fingering the rim of his hat as if in a hurry to be off. 'Accidents happen.' Then he grinned at her. 'Sometimes for the best.'

Her temper rose to think he thought she had enjoyed being incarcerated for two days and nights! Perhaps he thought she needed the sharp lesson to be more careful — he had warned her about the dangers to be found in the jungle. Then she remembered the effort he had made to rescue her.

Thinking he had postponed the search for her father's camp because of her ordeal, and because of her injured ankle, Frances said as he moved to leave the tent, 'When are we going on to meet my papa? I am recovered well enough now. You must not delay longer because of me. I can ride.'

George was half out of the tent, but came back to stand over her bed. 'I have sent guides and some mules ahead to find your father. They will report back to us, so do not worry about that.'

'Why are we staying here?'

He ran his fingers though his hair, grinning. 'Have you not been told? My dear girl.' His eyes glistened as he said triumphantly, 'Your fall has revealed a long-lost Mayan temple site!'

Frances looked puzzled.

He gave a laugh. 'This area was

inhabited by the Mayan tribes thousands of years ago. Many of their buildings have been found, but the jungle has covered many up. This area had a very important site that has been lost for centuries, and until you fell into the ruins of a building a few days ago, no one knew where it was in the vast jungle.'

Frances lay back on her cushions and suddenly chuckled. 'So my disaster was not such a disaster after all?'

'No, indeed. It has been a wonderful find, a marvellous success!'

Well, thought Frances crossly, *I wouldn't quite call my experience a success. It was horrible.* But she could understand why the others might see the discovery of an important Mayan site as wonderful.

Frances wanted to question him further about the exciting find, only she could see he was anxious to leave and get on with the excavation work. So she asked, 'Will you tell me about it later?'

'Of course. The Mexicans say it appears to be one of the best Mayan sites that has ever been discovered. We have sent for a team of labourers to help clear the site, which appears to be extensive. Now get some rest, and I will show you some of what has already been found later.'

He was gone. Frances was sad he had to go, but she knew he needed to leave her and get on with his work.

Encouraged that some good had come out of her suffering, Frances began to think positively. She had been told that some men, and the mules Papa needed, had been sent on to look for her father, so she did not have to worry about that either.

She determined that in future, she would do what she could to help with the excavation. Perhaps they would be glad if she would make some drawings of their finds.

Almost restored to her former confidence, Frances offered to help Maria with the camp chores.

'No, no, Mrs Webster! You must rest, Mr Webster says,' Maria told her firmly.

'I have another woman here now who can help me with the cooking.'

Frances was not sorry to hear that. If they were to remain here for some time, she could make some sketches — She gasped.

Where was her art equipment? She had it when she went into the jungle and fell beneath the earth — but where was it now?

'Have you seen my sketchbook?' she asked Maria as she was bringing her a meal into the tent.

Maria shook her head.

Frances was dismayed. She had lost her sketchbook — along with many of the Mexican flower drawings she had made in Veracruz. Her bag containing her art brushes and paints would have fallen down into the cave with her and it was depressing to think that even if her art work was found, it was most likely be wet and ruined!

While Frances attempted to shrug off her misfortune, unknown to her momentous events were unfolding around her.

A great historic site was being revealed.

George Webster confided to his man, Sam Stanley, 'I am no archaeologist, and have little knowledge of Mexican historic cultures, but I am certain we will find some significant Mayan treasures soon. The problem is, we did not expect to find this enormous site. We were going to a much smaller site where thefts have occurred. Now we are faced with a vast area to protect. What can we do to organise the men so that no one carelessly spoils anything that is found?'

'All we can do, sir, until reinforcements arrive, is to tell the diggers to be careful. And to watch out for thieves ourselves, now that the site has been made known — protect any valuable finds as best we can.'

'When are extra workmen expected?'

'They may have come already. Shall we go and see?'

As they moved along a narrow path that had been cleared a little wider with machetes towards the site, George, who was in front, asked, 'Did you send word to the Culture Minister?'

'Yes, he will be informed. The difficulty is that some of this site may be in Guatemala.'

Uneasy to think that the Mexican authorities, who had commissioned him to track down art thieves, may not realise the extent of this vast Mayan site, George was thinking the odds were against him. He feared thieves would attack the site before long. Dangerous men, who might destroy some precious artwork — but would also think nothing of harming men, as well as looting. He had been told a few greedy men had been successfully shipping Mayan treasure to Europe for profit, and must be stopped.

George had already begun to form some idea about how they accomplished their evil trade. He was aware that these thieves, like prowling wolves anxious to pounce, might already be circling around the campsite.

And, if that were not worry enough,

there was Miss Frances Cannon. An admirable young lady in many ways — but stubborn — and here in the jungle she was just another responsibility he could do without.

8

The following morning Frances awoke feeling better and was determined to be helpful. But as George had only crept into the tent late at night for a few hours' sleep before waking and dashing out once more, she did not have chance to ask him if there was anything he would like her to do.

Maria brought her breakfast and told her that more men had come to the camp to help with the dig, and the women were busy feeding them but had no need of assistance from her. Besides, her ankle was still sore to walk on; she soon found that out, when she gingerly put her foot on the ground.

Moving gently from her camp bed, she was able to hop around and see if she could find a spare sketchbook she might have brought with her. She needed a stick, and fortunately found she could use her furled parasol.

To her delight she did find another small sketchbook, a tiny paintbox and a pencil. Now she felt able to start again.

Everyone seemed too busy to notice her hobbling around the camp. The women were doing some washing down by the river or preparing vegetables for the midday meal. The men were not about and Frances thought they would be working, clearing the Mayan site. George was nowhere to be seen. But she had understood that Mayan sites could cover a square mile.

Finding a small area, only a step away from the camp clearing, amongst the tangle of plants, where she could sit in peace shaded by the canopy of tree leaves, Frances found an intriguing bijagua, a swinging flower with beautiful colouring, and began drawing.

Concentrating on her work, Frances was only half aware that people were calling and shouting. Then, when she became hungry, she packed up her things, thinking the midday meal must be ready to eat.

But she found everyone had gone!

She noticed the cooking pots left bubbling away on the camp fires, and wondered if they had assembled somewhere to eat. She knew since the discovery of the Mayan site there would be many areas around where everyone could have gone. Hampered by her inability to walk far, she felt exhausted, and soon gave up searching for them. She reasoned that the tents were still there, and they would return before long.

And yet . . . was she experiencing a slight sense of panic?

Why had she not told Maria where she'd hidden herself to draw?

The next moment, a big hand was cupped around her mouth and another around her waist. Before she knew what was happening, the strong person holding her had thrown her onto the ground.

She tried to scream, but the hand over her mouth prevented any more than a squeaking sound. Struggling to free herself from the grasp of the man holding her, she heard George hiss in her ear. 'Keep quiet, or you will get us both killed.'

'What . . . ?' she tried to ask as he removed his hand from her mouth.

'Hush! Quiet, I said.'

Having George with her was a relief. Despite the discomfort of being floored and held tightly by him, he was not hurting her. In fact, he seemed to be protecting her — but from what? Was there a tiger prowling that had frightened all the people away from the clearing?

He put his finger to his mouth to indicate she must be silent, then motioned with his hand that they were to crawl further into the jungle.

On her hands and knees she crawled after him, controlling a chuckle at the thought that if the sedate ladies of Bath could see her now — alone with a man, crawling around the jungle floor — they would probably have the vapours! Discomfort and indignities were all part of adventures, she reminded herself.

Having pushed their way into the undergrowth, George left her and peered out into the clearing.

'What are you looking for?' she whispered, putting her head near his.

'Get down, you idiot!'

Chastened to be called an idiot, Frances bit back a retort. Whatever it was that George was scared of was surely dangerous to her too. She held her tongue and tried to sit comfortably amongst the vegetation to rest her foot, ignoring any insects that might bite.

She noticed a tree on her right with sharp spikes sticking out — it was crawling with ants. She determinedly refused to look at it, although already she could imagine the ants crawling all over her!

Her clothes covered her well, she told herself, and there were far worse dangers about than a few creepy-crawlies.

Men's voices could be heard. Coming closer.

'Commandante!' She heard a man

call. Her heart thumped.

The men spoke in a language Frances did not understand. But it was obvious they were not friendly Indians because George had turned towards her, a finger on his lips and eyes commanding her to be quiet.

Danger had come to them. Were they the rebels she had heard about? Vicious men who might harm them?

Dangerous men or not, George had thought of her and had come to look for her. He was anxious to protect her. She was touched to think he cared.

Waiting in silence, Frances became aware that her ankle ached. She was hungry and had lost her artwork again. But she felt strengthened that she was with George. He turned to look at her every so often to nod reassuringly — and she was grateful for it.

It seemed to her an exceedingly long time before he leaned closer and murmured quietly, 'I think they have gone. But they may well come back.'

'Who are they?' Frances whispered,

flicking an ant off her gown.

Keeping his voice low he replied, 'We are not sure if they are rebels, or looters. The Indians warned us they were prowling around this area. They are a rough-looking lot and carry machetes, so it is best to hide from them. They have found our camp so we must lie low until reinforcements come.'

Nervously, she whispered, 'Who will come and protect us from them?'

'Government troops.'

Seeing the look of puzzlement on her face, he continued talking in a hushed voice. 'A message has been sent to the garrison in Veracruz. The Mexican government are anxious to protect their heritage. Too many ancient Mayan tombs have been looted in the past. Objects thoughtlessly destroyed by men only interested in stealing things to sell. Now the Mexican government wants archaeologists to examine any finds carefully and make records. That's why they will be sending soldiers as well as the art experts.'

Frances looked closely into his eyes. How beautiful they were; she felt she wanted to gaze into them forever. And he seemed to be comfortable studying her. After a moment or two she asked what she had wanted to know for some time. 'George, why did you come to Mexico? It was not for photography, was it?'

He now seemed willing to reveal his true mission. 'In part,' he replied. He listened for any sound of any of intruders still about, then continued softly, 'There has been unease amongst reputable art dealers in London for some time that collectors are obtaining items from looters. There is a gang operating from Veracruz, so I have been asked to investigate and stop this illegal trade.'

'Ah,' said Frances. 'So you are a police officer.'

'No.' He appeared amused. 'Not a police officer. I am a photographer.'

He went on quietly, 'Photography will become a vital tool to record ancient finds. It is a new science, still in its infancy. Any pictures we obtain at present are difficult to produce. But a distinguished scientist I know, William Fox Talbot, is experimenting to improve the process. He wanted me to try taking some photographs; people want to see pictures of the world. Fox Talbot is sure it will not be long before photographs can be taken more easily. Which would be marvellous for recording the ancient sites and where the objects are found.'

'Better than the work artists do?'

'No, just different. Artists are indispensable. They can record more than mere copies of things. Anyone can learn to take photographs — they do not have to be artistically skilled like you.'

It was kind of him to say so and Frances went pink. She said, 'Both methods can work well together.'

'Yes, I would say that is correct.' His beaming smile warmed her.

Her thoughts returning to the present, she asked in concern, 'Where are the others?'

'When an Indian came to warn us the armed men were coming towards our camp, our party took refuge in a nearby village. They told me they could not find you; that is why I came back to look for you.'

'I am sorry to have been a nuisance again.'

He frowned as he pursed his lips. Then he said, 'Frances, it is not your fault the rebels came this way. It is fortunate that you had got out of bed and were out of sight.'

She did not have to ask why a woman found alone would have been in danger from a group of rebel soldiers. So she asked, 'Do the rebels often use the jungle trails?'

'I do not know. It is not known how many rebels, bandits or criminals there are hidden in the jungles. They usually avoid the Indian villages because they know the Indians are good fighters. But our camp is an unarmed group and they can steal anything they want from us.'

Frances shivered. He did not seem to notice, or maybe he was pleased he had got her to understand how vulnerable she was in the jungle. He went on, 'And to add to our troubles we are on the border between Mexico and Guatemala. So there are Guatemalan villains to contend with too.'

'Oh dear!'

He smiled as he winked at her. 'Do you wish you were back at Veracruz, having a leisurely time at the hotel?'

'No indeed! That would bore me to tears.'

'But it would be safer.'

She took a long breath in. 'But think what I would miss seeing. Having the experiences of a lifetime.'

'Including being married to me?'

For a few moments their eyes met again. Nothing was said, but Frances was strangely moved by his candid stare. He did not appear to be teasing her, and to her astonishment he leaned over and quickly gave her a gentle kiss on her cheek.

Thrown into a state of confusion as well as pleasure by the touch of his lips, she raised her hand to stroke the side of his whiskery face.

He slid his arm around her, drawing her nearer, and placed his lips lightly on hers, sending a thrilling sensation throughout her body. He drew back immediately afterwards, muttering, 'I think not . . .'

She did not want him to let her go, but knew he was right to be aware that this was not the time to embrace. Danger was around them and they must be on guard. Thankful he was there with her, she murmured, 'I do not find being called Mrs Webster at all disagreeable.'

He chuckled.

Frances felt her mouth dry and longed for a drink. 'I am thirsty,' she said.

'So am I. But I dare not venture out of this hiding place unarmed.' He sighed. 'It was stupid of me not to think of bringing a gun when I came to look for you. Stanley and I brought some guns with us, but my men took them to the village.'

'I have a gun in my tent,' Frances remarked brightly.

'You have a gun?'

'Indeed. Colonel Washburton lent me his when he knew I was going on this expedition to find my father.'

'What kind of gun is it?'

Frances shrugged. 'I know nothing about guns.'

George's amused eyes were looking intently at her. 'Well, describe it.'

'He said it was a pistol. The colonel said he used it when he went tiger shooting in India.'

'Have you any bullets for it?'

She looked at him, astonished. 'Of course I have! I was shown how to use it — although I am hopeless at shooting at a target.'

George laughed. 'I was not thinking of you doing any shooting, Frances. I would like the pistol — just in case. And believe me, I can shoot straight.'

She believed him. 'Well, you will have to go into my tent and look for it,' she said. 'You should find it easily enough, I only have two saddlebags.'

George got to his feet and stretched his tall body. 'That is if the rebels haven't already taken it.'

'Yes, I suppose they might . . . only I put it amongst my underclothes and I do not suppose the men would be bothered to look there.'

George gave her a wry grin. 'Do not move from here. I will be back soon,' he told her, stepping away so that the leaves closed behind him and Frances was left all alone.

It was a new anxiety that gripped Frances after he had left. Having overcome her claustrophobic feelings of being in the jungle, and the humid heat, then learning to respect the dangers of straying into the undergrowth, she now had the added fear of knowing that evil men roamed nearby.

But even more than her own safety, she felt alarmed for George, because now she knew she not only admired him — she trusted him. She loved him. She had found a treasure of her own!

And she had discovered he was on official business to stop art trafficking, and feared he might be a target for looters. Her only comfort was that government soldiers were on their way to protect them.

9

When George returned — after a long time in which Frances was almost frantic worrying about him — he was struggling to carry two cumbersome saddlebags. He also brought an oilcloth and a water bottle.

He gave her quick grin. 'Sorry if I worried you, taking so long. I was being cautious. I was unsure if there were any intruders around, so I had to creep about.'

Frances wiped a tear from her face and gave him a brave smile. He dropped the bags and offered her a drink, which she accepted gratefully.

'Fortunately,' he said, 'I do not think any unwelcome visitors are still prowling around — although they may return. But I think we are safer staying here until we know for sure they have moved on.'

'Will they come back?'

'If they do not, others may. Once these gangs get wind of a find of the magnitude we have here, we will be in constant danger of being attacked.'

He was taking out a ground sheet and seemed to give his attention to trying to unwrap it in the confined space. She helped him, remarking, 'You do not seem too concerned.'

'Oh, but I am, I assure you. As a government investigator there are always criminals wanting to get rid of me.'

Horrified, Frances dropped the corner of the oilskin. 'But why?'

He carried on with the task of laying the groundsheet flat saying, 'Because I know too much.'

'But how can these rebels, looters, or whatever they are, know that?'

'I suspect some of these men may have infiltrated our camp.'

A shiver ran down Frances's back. 'No!'

'Oh, indeed. It is a dangerous assignment I am on.'

Frances went rigid. 'Then why did you take it?'

He grinned. 'I might ask you the same question. Why did you come here, when you had been warned of the dangers?'

'But that is not the same.'

'My dear girl, it is exactly the same. You have your goals. I have mine. We were both willing to risk danger to get what we want.'

Frances could not deny that. He had to seek thieves; she, her father.

He gave a little laugh. 'So here we are. We are stuck with it. Let us get this cover over us before we get soaked. Rain is on the way. And when it rains here, it sloshes down.'

Frances realised they had similar natures, and had to accept that the only way they were going to get out of their predicament was to proceed with their aims and not allow fear of the dangers that might befall them to stop them.

He placed her bag near her, saying, 'I do not believe they rifled through our things. I brought one of my saddlebags and one of yours — but I did not know which one to bring, so I hope I chose the one with things in that you might find useful.'

'Very kind of you,' she said giving him another smile. She could not think of anything she needed at that moment — except him, and all she could do was to try and control her imagination, which was full of qualms.

'That is what I like about you,' he remarked. 'You are such a practical young lady. No vapours, no complaining and no fear — '

'George, I am not the courageous lady you think I am! I love exploring the world, but I now know how dangerous the jungle can be — especially when I know armed gangs are near our camp. I am terrified.'

He looked at her sharply. 'Well, you never look it!' He then gave her a warm, reassuring smile. 'In any case, are not we all scared at times?'

She was glad he considered that she

showed presence of mind in a crisis. She was also pleased to know he felt vulnerable at times too. It made him a man with sensitivity — who would appreciate the finer things in life.

But now she was worried about their safety. 'Did you find the gun?'

'I did. And I hope we do not have to use it, because it would be better in a museum.'

Frances stiffened. 'Does it not work?'

George, who was unpacking his bag, drew out a mosquito net ready to cover them saying, 'I expect it will — I'm only teasing you.'

Frances bit back her retort that with the area crawling with machete-carrying rebels, it was not the time to joke about whether the only firearm they had worked or not. But then she realised she had told George she was frightened, and he was only trying to calm her fears by being light-hearted.

He looked around and pointed to the wide foot of a giant ceiba tree. 'Let's sit here. We can rest our backs against the tree trunk. I brought this oilcloth because a chipi chipi is just starting.'

'Chipi chipi?'

'It's what they call rain here. Light rain. But it may torrent down as well. You cannot feel it yet because we are under the canopy of the leaves from the trees, but soon we shall be drenched if we do not make a shelter fast.'

'Shall we put up my parasol and cover it with the oilcloth?'

'Excellent idea — provided you do not mind snuggling up to me?'

Frances considered it for a moment. Why should she mind nestling up to him? She loved him, and no one need ever know. 'Well, we are supposed to be married,' she replied with a giggle.

Finding a wide niche between the buttresses at the base of the tree, they sat close together, drawing the mosquito net and oilskin over them. Frances revelled in the feeling of security she had from being in close proximity to the man she loved.

After a few minutes, the drips of rain

became steadier and they were glad to be covered by their tiny tent.

'Lord, I am hungry,' said George, and his stomach rumbled to prove the point. 'I brought nothing for us to eat.'

'I have some carrots in my saddle-bag.'

George turned to look at her questioningly.

'I got them for my mule — he needed a little encouragement at times.'

'No wonder your bag was so heavy to carry!'

'I am known for my eccentricity.'

As George pushed her saddlebag nearer for her to open, he replied, 'You, odd? Heavens, no! You are an attractive young lady — a most desirable and ingenious young woman.'

Frances blushed. She had received a good deal of praise for her art, but had never received such a personal compliment from a gentleman before.

With his help she managed to open her saddlebag and took out a couple of large orange carrots, one each, and they crunched them in harmony.

'Have you had any more news of my father?' she asked as she chewed.

He swallowed. 'No, but I hope to get news very soon.' He took a large bite out of his carrot.

She stopped chewing and asked, 'What if the rebels attack his camp?'

George swallowed. 'I should not imagine he would have anything the rebels would want to steal. And as you tell me he has been working here for two or three years, I doubt he is in any more danger now than a year ago.'

He sat munching the last of his carrot. Then he lay back, immediately closed his eyes and fell into a deep sleep.

Frances felt his head fall against her and was glad of his warm body next to her as she heard his steady breathing. Although far from having the comfort of home, and being in a compromising situation, she felt strangely content. It felt right that they should be together, and she had no worries about moving nearer him and letting her fingers tenderly feel his sleeping face. She wished he had kissed her again before he fell asleep. She had never dreamed how delightful it would be to have a man embrace her.

She heard some howler monkeys from afar, and screeching of parrots, but their calls were familiar now. It was not long before she was asleep too.

* * *

Stiffly she awoke next morning and stretched her long limbs. George had gone. But a scribbled message was on her sketchbook:

Will be back soon. Stay where you are and look after yourself. George.

The message was brief, but it meant a great deal to Frances, feeling as she did that she and George had formed a closer relationship. He was now very important to her, not only because she trusted him to get her out of the jungle alive, but because she feared for his safety as much as her own.

Getting to her feet she found her ankle less sore, and she felt she had become a different person. No, perhaps not a different person; it was that she had come to realise she could be herself. George had told her she was an attractive young woman; not eccentric as she had been led to believe. She was unusually tall, but so was he. She liked to travel; so did he. And he had told her that feeling afraid was to be expected in some situations, so she need not pretend to be daring. Even falling in love was not something she was incapable of. Indeed, she had fallen head over heels!

Hearing voices, she held her breath for a moment. But she listened carefully and recognised women's high-pitched chatter. She guessed the rebels had moved on or had been chased away. It was a relief. But looking down at the state of her gown — she could only imagine her tangled hair! How she longed to get washed and tidied up.

Gingerly she poked her head out of the leaves to look at the camp clearing. It all seemed quite calm and everyone was going about their work as usual.

Ashamed to be so dishevelled and still hobbling on her sore ankle, Frances managed to find her way back to her tent without attracting too much attention. The women were busy clearing up after having to leave the camp in a hurry the day before.

Having refreshed herself with a wash and change of clothes, she was delighted to be offered breakfast.

'Mr Webster said you are hungry this morning so I cook you much coffee, tortillas and two eggs.'

'Thank you, Maria. Is Justo safe?'

'Oh yes, Mrs Webster, everyone is safe. My husband, he is looking after the mules. They must be watered and fed too.'

Frances was pleased no one had come to any harm after the raid. And, strangely, she now felt quite delighted to be known as Mrs Webster.

'The rebels did no much damage,' Maria told her. 'They took a few things and ate the meal we were cooking, then left.'

'You are too good a cook, Maria!' Frances teased her.

When George returned for the *comida* — or midday meal — he chose to sit by Frances, and returned her smile. He told her, between mouthfuls of food, that they could not go on to find her father yet, because he was worried that their discovery of the Mayan site may have been noticed by the rebels, and that armed looters may soon hear about the find and come to steal what they could — so they must stay and protect the site as best they could until reinforcements arrive.

'In the meantime,' he chewed and swallowed, 'careful records must be kept of what is being discovered.'

Frances had already guessed that job needed to be done. She asked him to tell her about the progress of the excavation work.

'We have a fair idea of the extent of the site,' he explained. 'It has a towering palace and an enormous pyramid tomb — I will show you, though there is much clearing work to be done before it can be seen properly.'

'I should love to see it,' murmured Frances. 'Perhaps I can do some drawing for you?'

His eyes gleamed appreciatively. 'That would be helpful. I cannot take photographs with insufficient light, and I have little equipment with me.'

George left her abruptly and came back with a few glass plates with photographs of some sections of the ruins that had been revealed. He reminded her with a playful nudge that he was not able to bring all the equipment he needed — because she had taken all the pack animals!

Frances was amazed seeing the photographs. They were magical images the way they recorded exactly what one could see, although they were dull.

'I am sure I can help you with

recording more details,' said Frances, keen both to be useful and to see the wonderful Mayan remains.

'That would be appreciated,' he said, and looking quickly around to see no one was looking, he gave her a brief kiss.

Frances felt ecstatic.

★ ★ ★

The day-by-day life in the camp resumed. Extra tents were set up for the influx of men who arrived to help with the work of uncovering the ancient city. The excavation site became a hive of workers. Not only workers to dig, but soldiers to guard them, and amongst them archaeologists from Mexico City. Advances were quickly made revealing the lost Mayan city.

Excitement ran through the camp as each important find was revealed. And the expectation of more valuable finds spurred them on in the hot conditions, which were not conducive to physical work.

George and Stanley rigged up their cumbersome photographic equipment, and began the slow process of taking more rather bleary pictures of the finds.

Frances was able to work much more quickly and soon managed to make many excellent drawings of what was unearthed. Crawling down into tombs and with the light from lanterns, lit and held for her by Stanley, she recorded the layout of the found objects. The red cinnabar drawings, patterns and picture writing she carefully copied, and vessels she drew in the position they were found.

Everyone was most impressed when she showed them what she had done at the end of each day. She was thrilled to find she was being of use to the archaeologists. But most of all she was thrilled that her drawings pleased George, who said, 'Not only do you draw most skilfully, Frances, you manage to capture the essence of the Mayan civilisation. Well done!'

Even seeing so little of him, the

precious moments when they were alone seemed to fill her mind.

Frances was so absorbed with her work she almost forgot about looking for her father, until one evening when she was told they would be moving on next day to find him.

'What will happen to the excavation work?' she asked George as they sat talking after the evening meal. 'You are so interested in it.'

George put down his cup, and whispered, 'It's true I regret having to leave here, as I do find it exciting unearthing the past. But the work here will carry on and one day I hope to return. I promised your aunt and uncle to find Professor Cannon, so I must. Then my next task is not here; it is at Veracruz. I have to infiltrate the network of thieves. I have to discover who steals the relics, and the route they take to get them illegally into London salerooms.'

'Things from this site?'

George gave her a wink. 'Yes. Sam Stanley and I have deliberately planned to allow a few things to go missing — a fine jade death mask from a tomb, and a carved jade necklace. We hope to trace the thieves when they attempt to smuggle them on board a ship sailing to England.'

Frances thought that a good idea, but asked, 'What exactly is jade?'

'Jade is precious stone. Fine green jade is rare, and difficult to mine. It is an extremely hard and durable stone. The best stone is very beautiful. It was considered very valuable by the ancient Mayans, more so than gold or silver, so their most skilled craftsmen have carved the jade objects we find.'

Frances listened, fascinated. When George fished a bright green bead out of his pocket, she gazed at it with reverence. 'I am amazed by the skilled carving on this tiny piece of jewellery. To think it was made so long ago.'

'Indeed,' said George gravely. 'This large site shows a magnificent city was thriving here thousands of years ago. It is marvellous what the Mayans achieved. However it is essential for the Mexicans to protect these remains. More guards are expected here tomorrow, and when they come we will be off to find your father's camp.'

'Will my father not be in Veracruz by now?'

'He may be. But just in case he is struggling with his long mule train, I thought it would be wise for us to ride over to where he had his camp. Then we can make sure he has left and is on route back towards Villahermosa.'

The thought of going further along miles of hilly tracks, through tangled branches and leaves of the jungle, no longer had the same attraction for Frances as before — she was too aware of possible dangers. However, she did want to make sure her father was safely on his way home.

Anticipating travelling with George was exciting, though. She felt she wanted to be with him always.

10

They had been travelling for several days, along narrow tracks in dense green jungle with the mules hauling their riders up and down the foothills — and Frances, when she forgot the dangers they could face, loved it.

'This ride is wonderful,' she remarked to George one day during a rest period. 'The forest is so full of beauty — I shall remember it all my life.'

George smiled at her. 'It's damn hot. Think about it; you could be strolling in the gentle breeze in a park like most young ladies in Bath.'

Frances smiled back. It was perfectly true she could be in Bath, enjoying temperate weather. But even in England, rainy days and heat waves occurred at times — and it was not as exciting as being in South America, with new sounds and sights to enjoy. She did not like to say she would not be with him if she were in Bath, so she merely replied, 'True, but I can saunter around parks and admire the flower beds when I am an old lady.'

George laughed. 'You will never become an old lady if you do not keep away from dangers.'

'Nevertheless, I prefer to live adventurously — it is more fun.'

He chuckled, but then looked at her sharply. 'To some extent, I agree. But real danger is not amusing. I would have thought your taste of it when we lost you would have cured your appetite for taking risks.'

She thought for a moment. 'I must admit I made a mistake, not thinking how easy it was to get lost so near the path. I was very scared, and I would not like to have another experience like it. But, it has not deterred me from exploring. Despite the discomforts and possible dangers I would still like to see more of the world's beauty.'

He nodded and gave her a broad

smile. 'Frances, I believe you are like me, with an insatiable appetite for seeing the world.'

'Indeed I must be.' Frances nodded. 'Ouch!' she then exclaimed, slapping her face. 'I have been bitten again.' A mosquito had managed to crawl under her hat net and had bitten her cheek.

'That is the trouble with travel. Something is inclined to bite you every so often. Just be thankful it was not a vampire bat,' remarked George.

'There are none of those about, surely.'

'Oh yes there are — they live in this jungle.'

Frances grimaced. She knew he was too occupied looking for more serious signs of potential danger to wish to converse for long. She considered seeing the colourful parrots and toucans, the antics of the monkeys, and all the amazing plants she was noticing in the thick of the jungle well worth having to suffer a few trivial hardships.

Her ankle now much improved,

Frances once again assisted the capable Maria in the task of feeding the men when they found a clearing in which to camp for the night.

'You make a good wife, Mrs Webster,' remarked Maria as they chatted over the cooking.

Frances watched the steam rise from the pot she was stirring. At home her mama had maids to do the housework, and she had not learned any cooking or laundry skills until the Mexican woman showed her how it was done. Challenged to do as well as the Mexican women, Frances had soon become capable, and enjoyed some physical work after a day's sitting drawing, or riding her mule.

'I do not suppose my mama would like to have bean soup and tacos for dinner every day,' she said with a little laugh. 'In England we have roast beef, ragouts, pies and puddings. There are bakers to make bread and muffins and pastry cooks to make fruit tarts.'

Now it was Maria's turn to give a

chuckle. 'Now I know why you have grown so tall!'

Frances laughed happily. Before she came to Mexico she might have felt extremely unhappy to be reminded of her height. But with George even taller than herself, she did not mind now being taller than most women.

George continued treating her as a friend. One evening they chatted before they slept in their camp beds, cocooned in their mosquito nets. George mentioned that they would be out of the jungle very soon and he thought she would be glad to get back to the comforts of home life.

'Oh no!' Frances exclaimed. 'It is true I have a comfortable home, and a kind mama. And when papa is at home, he has work for me to do. But,' she added wistfully, 'I realise now I was lonely in Bath at times. I suppose it is my fault because I detested the ordinary occupations of women. Sewing, tea parties and shopping expeditions bore me. I much prefer to be here.'

George laughed. 'You are indeed a true female explorer.'

'I suppose I am. Mama hopes I will settle down. And one day, perhaps, I will — but only after several years of exciting travel.'

'Mmm. Me too.'

Frances was curious and wondered whether he wanted to ask her if she wanted to marry eventually and have a family, as most women did. She longed to know if he had the same plan. But considering he might think it too forward of her to ask, she questioned him about his family instead.

'My father is an engineer,' he told her. 'He builds bridges and is working for the well-known engineer, Mr Brunel. They are constructing the new railways and tunnels. I have three brothers and two sisters.'

This made Frances, who was an only child, wonder what family life was like. 'What fun it must be for you to have a big family,' she said wistfully.

'Yes,' he said a little uncertainly.

Quick to catch the hesitation in his voice, she asked, 'You sound a little unsure. Have you a disagreement with your family?'

Clearly he had, because he did not deny it.

'Of course families have quarrels at times,' she said reassuringly. 'I have argued with my mama because she is an elegant society lady, and I am not. But these disagreements blow over.'

'Not mine, alas,' he replied.

'Why not tell me about it? 'she asked softly, sensing he was not at peace, and that he might find sharing his sorrow with her some consolation.

She heard him turn over on his camp bed. For a while she felt she had probed too deeply and he would not confide in her, but after a few moments he began. 'Unlike my brothers, who became engineers like my father, I decided I was interested in travel, archaeology and photography.'

Taking a deep breath before continuing, as if it was an effort for him to

146

speak, he said, 'I read all I could, joined societies and met several eminent explorers, archaeologists and scientists — and I travelled abroad to see some famous sites.'

As he fell silent Frances, sensing he had more to tell, prompted him by saying, 'Why should your family dislike your chosen occupation?'

He snorted. 'They did not. But unfortunately when I took a job with an art dealer to learn more about the collecting, buying and selling of antiques, I was accused of embezzlement.'

Frances held her breath.

There was a pause before he continued rather hoarsely, 'I was sent for trial. Jailed — and thereby shamed my family.'

Frances gasped. 'Did you steal anything?'

'I did not!'

There was a touch of anger in his voice, and she regretted having asked the question. She knew in her heart that he was an honest, decent man.

After she remained silent he continued, 'I was soon set free. They found the thief. They said it was all a terrible mistake and offered me my job back. But I was devastated. Unable to go back to work with those who had so quickly called me a villain . . . they had ruined my reputation . . . I might well have been stuck in prison for years for a crime I did not commit. In any case, all I wished to do when I was released was to get away from them all. Including my family.'

'How dreadful,' said Frances, genuinely shocked, 'that you had to suffer so, when it was all a terrible mistake. But why did your family not rally to support you?'

'They may have tried. I do not know. But my arrest happened so quickly. When you are suddenly taken into custody it is difficult . . . I was not visited by anyone in prison. I presumed my family were ashamed of me.

'Then one day I was told I was free to leave — but I did not know what to do, where to go. I was angry too, because my family had shunned me.'

Frances felt tears in her eyes. She could now understand why he had been so aloof and uncommunicative when she had first met him. 'How awful it must have been for you!' she murmured.

'It was dreadful.' He was talking freely now about the horrible experience that had been inflicted on him, and she listened, amazed to learn how destroyed he must have felt. 'I had little money. No work. I did not want to go and beg from my family. But with the help of friends, I survived. Then I met William Fox Talbot, who is a great scientist, and I became interested in his discovery of photography. I visited him at Laycock Abbey and he and his assistants showed me his methods, which I told him could be used to record archaeological finds. He paid for me to travel to Mexico and try out his photographic equipment.'

Frances cringed, thinking that because

she had taken all the mules, he could not bring all the equipment he needed. No wonder he had been cross with her.

George continued, 'Then, when I was about to set sail, I was asked by the police to investigate the smuggling of works of art from Mexico. I said I would, because I was angry about being unjustly imprisoned for what these people did. I wanted them caught, but felt I had no chance of nailing them. Then a retired officer, Sam Stanley, came forward and offered to help me with the undercover investigation. He told me he had worked for Scotland Yard, so I was pleased to have his assistance.'

Frances could understand why George was glad to have a knowledgeable companion. Though, remembering Stanley often sitting smoking alone, she thought it a pity he was not more of a companion. But then, she reasoned, he was supposed to be George's manservant, and therefore would remain aloof.

She was glad to know the truth about

George, and admired the difficulties he had overcome. She felt humbled. He was a man who had suffered unjustly. She understood him better now that he had opened his heart to her, and felt she respected and trusted him. His presence had brought enrichment into her life.

She left her bed and went over to his, raising the mosquito net. Taking his well-formed hand, she pressed it to her lips. He turned to her and smiled. Then his lips melted with hers briefly.

'Now you have told me about your pain, you can put it behind you George,' she said softly.

'Ugh! I wish that were true.'

Frances asked urgently, 'Why can you not?'

He swung his legs off the bed and got up to look out of the tent entrance. 'Because it is not over yet. I have to be constantly vigilant. Stanley and I feel sure that some of the Indians in our party are, sadly, untrustworthy.'

Alarmed, Frances returned to her

camp bed and, seating herself, asked, 'Can Justo not help you?'

He looked across at her. 'I am trying to keep Justo and his wife out of this investigation. I hired them only to look after you.'

Frances appreciated the burden of responsibilities George was carrying as he went on, 'Even when we get to Veracruz, I have to be on the alert for the criminals who may attack me for wanting to put a stop to their illicit trade. Then, if I survive, I have to find somewhere to live, ignoring my family — or constantly travel the world.'

Appalled at the way he saw his future, Frances cried, 'I am sure you have more options than that!'

'For example?'

'Well, I think that you could marry. Settle down with a woman who understands your previous difficulties, and helps you to overcome them.' Then having said exactly what was in her mind, Frances blushed a deep crimson at her forthrightness — thankful to be hidden by her mosquito net.

'Hmm. No lady would want an ex-jailbird.'

'I think that misfortune would not be held against you.'

He gave a little laugh. 'Society can be most unfair at times, Frances.'

Frances knew from experience that some people could condemn others from their ranks far too easily. A woman like herself, who spent nights with a man — however innocently — was not eligible in society's eyes either.

Disappointed that he said nothing to remove the stigma on her for having been labelled his wife, or to assure her that the circumstances which had led to their 'marriage' did not condemn her, she felt a tear creep down her cheek. She thought it a shame when he simply put his feet up on his bed and slept immediately so they could not discuss anything further.

She tossed and turned on her bed, feeling rejected, before she too slept.

Not everyone in the camp was asleep that night. Soon after the midnight hour, as the nocturnal animals prowled looking for prey, two shifty-eyed Indians removed the blankets covering them and crept out of their tent. It was not entirely dark in the clearing. Enough light for them to see and move quickly and silently, without using lanterns.

Going to the packs, which had been removed from the mules' backs during the night to rest the animals, they soon located the cloth bundles containing objects they were looking for. All they did was to remove one bundle from a pack and put it into another.

In the dim light, two eyes watched them from the undergrowth, and a twisted smile spread over the watcher's face as he observed the deed being done. How easy it was now for the valuable objects to be shipped to England. The watcher waited for the Indians to return to their tent before he slipped back into his.

In the morning when George noticed the bundle of treasures missing, he was satisfied — now he was sure about what he had suspected: a couple of thieves were travelling with them.

But his mission to find out who was behind the criminal activity had become even more dangerous. His enemies could strike at him at any time. He just hoped to get Frances, Maria and Justo to safety before anything happened to him.

Looking down, he gave a shiver when he saw a large insect with claws and a long tail curled back over its body, and recognised it was a scorpion with a poisonous sting. The Mayas called it the Sign of the Death-God.

Was it a warning?

The Mayan gods might indeed be warning him, but they must know he was no enemy of the Mayan people. His intention was to protect the Mayan treasures — not to steal them.

11

They did not go all the way to where Professor Arthur Cannon had been camped, because as they came near, they learned that the site had been abandoned.

'How will we know if my father has arrived safely out of the jungle?' Frances asked George anxiously as they sat together one evening watching the flames of the campfire burn low.

'I shall take you to Villahermosa to make sure. And when we find him I shall have to leave you.'

She asked in a hushed voice, 'Have you been able to discover who in our party is treacherous?'

George started, as if he had forgotten he had told Frances his suspicion that some Indians were thieves. 'Shush! Please do not even think about my investigation — it is far too dangerous.'

Frances regarded his worried expression and nodded.

'I know you can be a stubborn woman. Determined when you want something — and perhaps that is not always a bad thing.'

They smiled at each other.

'But,' he said, running his fingers through his hair, 'because I care about you and wish no harm to come to you ... ' Looking embarrassed, he stared at the fire. 'But things are complicated ... '

As his voice trailed off, Frances knew what he was trying to say. That he might be considering not just ending their sham marriage — but offering a real one.

Although she wished with all her heart that there was nothing blocking the happiness of their being in love, she knew she had to support his decision for them to part. 'George, you need not explain. I understand. I wish I could help you.'

He looked at her, searching. 'You

have helped me by listening to my tale of woe. It was a relief to be able to admit my secret past to someone, and to be able to step away from it — which I now feel I can do. So I thank you.'

'I have to thank you, too,' she said quickly. 'You have been a great 'husband' to me, and I will never forget your kindly protection. But I do not wish to lose your friendship.'

Smiling at her, he moved nearer and kissed her lightly and quickly. His eyes rested on hers as long as they could as he walked away.

Frances wept in her heart. She was not able to tell him how precious he had become to her — it was necessary for them both to hide the depth of their affection.

An unknown menace was keeping them apart. George hinted that he may know where it was — but she did not. She had the unsettling feeling that even when they left the jungle the danger would not be over.

They arrived at Villahermosa just as a cyclone hit the small town. Heavy clouds, swirling, mighty winds and drenching rain made the shelter of the hotel rooms and stables for the mules very welcome.

Although Frances was thankful to be inside a sturdy building, walking about in rooms and eating at a table seemed odd to her after being hemmed in by great trees and plants for many weeks.

She learned her father had passed through the town a week ago. Many people remembered him as a distinguished-looking European, and remarked on the very long mule train he had.

Professor Cannon had gone on to Veracruz, she was told, and George explained, 'I must leave you here now. As soon as the rain stops I shall travel on with the mule train, but I will arrange for a carriage to take you back to your family in Veracruz tomorrow, with Maria and Justo.'

Bravely, Frances accepted George had good reason to leave. She would have preferred a slow ride back along the coastal road to Veracruz with him — although it would have taken several days. But she was longing to see her father again, and George seemed anxious to get her back with her family quickly. Therefore, she did not argue, though it was painful to say goodbye.

Sleeping alone in her hotel bedroom, she missed George's presence — more than she could have imagined she would. It was an acute pain for her to be without him.

★　★　★

Upon her arrival at the hotel at Veracruz, it was wonderful to see her white-whiskered papa again. He looked happy, and she wondered why she had been so worried about him. He seemed delighted to see her, too.

Hugging him, Frances noticed how thin he had become, and thought how

160

Mama's cook would soon fatten him up again when he got home.

'Wonderful orchids I've found,' he declared. 'The orchid species seem endless.' He rattled on about them with great enthusiasm until Frances laughingly begged him to stop.

When she saw her Uncle William looking well again, she was so pleased.

Aunt Gina explained, 'William took a turn for the better soon after you left. He is quite well now, although I think he should take life easier in future.'

Frances could see Uncle William had lost some of his vigour, and having spent an exciting life exploring the world, she felt he probably would be content to retire to a more sedate life in Bath.

'Now I want you to tell us all about your expedition,' said Aunt Gina.

It was fun that evening, sitting with her family talking and laughing, comparing stories of their adventures. Frances felt like a seasoned traveller. But there was something missing from her enjoyment — George was not there.

She kept thinking, *where is he?* How much nicer it would be if he were amongst them, joining in the conversation and laughter.

Maria came up to her. 'Mrs Webster,' she said. 'I have put your things in room number seven.'

'Thank you, Maria,' said Frances wondering why everyone had suddenly become rather quiet. After Maria had bustled out, Aunt Gina's eyebrows rose as she turned to her niece. 'Did I hear her say *Mrs Webster?*'

The silence in the room, and the fixed stare of everyone towards her, made Frances blush deeply. 'I er, yes,' she said, uncomfortably struggling for words. 'You see, we thought it best . . . ' She looked down at her hand where Maria's ring was still on her finger. She had become so used to wearing it, she had forgotten to take it off.

Her father murmured, 'It is about time that Frances was married. Congratulations, my dear. I hope I shall like your husband.'

Uncle William boomed, 'Are you telling us you have gone and married that photography fellow?'

'No, I am not married,' Frances proclaimed promptly. 'It's just that I had to pretend I was. I had to sleep . . . use the same tent . . . ' She stopped speaking, realising her denial, and the explanation she had begun, seemed to put her in a worse position.

Taking pity on her red-faced, confused niece, Aunt Gina said quickly, 'I'm sure Frances will be able to explain more to us later.'

Frances certainly could not have said anything more at that time. But when the men rose to go and get a drink at the bar, her tongue loosened and she was able to tell her aunt all about George and her false marriage.

Aunt Gina was amused. She laughed heartily about Frances' predicament. 'Well,' she chuckled, 'you have certainly had plenty of experiences now, my dear.'

'You do not think I have ruined my

marriage chances, then?'

Aunt Gina's face became thoughtful for a moment or two, then she whispered to her worried niece, 'I should say, you have probably strengthened them!'

Frances could not think why this could be. However, Gina's face showed Frances she was not critical of her temporary 'marriage'. Gina had travelled for years and knew that although women had to be protected, they could not expect all the niceties to be given them in foreign lands.

But now the search had ended and the party had to prepare to return to England. Frances hoped every hour that she might get a message from George to say where he was and what he was doing. But she did not.

'We are sailing to Liverpool next week,' she was told by her aunt, 'so we shall have to start packing.'

Disappointed they might have to leave before she had heard from George, Frances was determined not to make a fuss. She presumed George was busy doing his job of tracking down the Mexican art looters. Instead of saying farewell to him, she had to be content with saying a loving goodbye to Maria and Justo — and leave a message for George with them.

She worried constantly about George's safety, and prayed that no harm came to him.

12

The City of Bath appeared serene to Frances after her exciting adventure to South America. The city's grand architecture, with the sunshine playing on the golden stone buildings that surrounded her were a complete contrast to the shaded wild green foliage of the jungle. The rustle of the city trees and the gentle birdsong were in vast contrast to the wild cries of howler monkeys.

In days past, arrivals at Bath appeared in the local newspapers. Frances thought her father deserved to be honoured for his work and had imagined a paragraph printed in the Bath Journal, stating: *Professor Arthur Cannon arrived back in Bath from the jungles of South America, on Wednesday, May 4th, 1846, having collected a great number of rare orchids, obtained* in *dangerous circumstances, for the Botanical Gardens at Kew. And his daughter, Miss Frances Cannon, was able to bring back many fine plant drawings she made in Mexico.*

However, their welcome was less spectacular.

'I'm overjoyed to see you back safe,' her mama cried with joy as she greeted and kissed her husband warmly, and then her daughter.

'Why Frances,' exclaimed her mother excitedly, 'you are changed — for the better, I can see! How well your hair is dressed — you must tell me how this came about.'

Frances was delighted to hear her mama's approval of her looks.

However, Mama was not interested in hearing all the details about their experiences in Mexico, although she was pleased with the plants and seeds they brought back. 'I shall watch them grow,' she said, but went on to say, 'Arthur, you look quite worn out. You are not to go away again.'

Professor Arthur Cannon kissed his wife again affectionately. 'Yes, my dear, I am very tired. I'm delighted with the studies I was able to make and specimens I have brought back, but I think you are right, I shall not go a roaming again.'

His wife sighed with pleasure.

The professor continued, 'I have aches and pains I did not suffer until recently. I need to slow down. The Horticultural Society can find a younger man to go abroad and search for new specimens. Besides, I have brought back enough to work on for years — with the help of Frances, who is excellent at cataloguing my finds.' He turned and beamed at his daughter.

Frances smiled back at her father. She had noticed that he had aged after his lengthy expedition, and considered he had made the right decision to remain with Mama from now on. He, and Uncle William, could play chess, and reminisce about their past travels like the older men they had become.

'Yes indeed, Frances will help me with the plants I have brought back,' her father repeated. 'I want them all carefully drawn — and no one draws them better than Frances.'

Delighted to hear her father's approval of her artistic ability, Frances said she would be happy to do any botanical drawings and paintings — although she slightly resented his dependence on her for being his secretary as well.

She ventured, 'I think, Papa, you will need to hire someone to help you besides myself.'

'Why? You are all I need.'

Frances pursed her lips. 'But, Papa, assisting you with your work is more than I have time to do. I have my painting. And other things . . . '

Both of her parents turned at once to regard her in great astonishment.

'Yes,' Frances continued boldly. 'I need some time to enjoy myself.'

Her mama questioned, 'What are you going to do?'

For want of any other excuse,

Frances smiled at her mother, saying, 'Well, I should like to go shopping in Bristol with you, and visit friends.'

Mrs Cannon was amazed to hear this from her changed, more elegant daughter, and persuaded her husband to look for a secretary.

Frances was pleased to think she had worthwhile occupations ahead of her and knew she should be entirely happy to be home with her family again. But, of course, she was not. George was constantly on her mind. And she was disappointed she had not heard from him. No matter how much she told herself that he would be a pleasant memory — her first love. No, indeed — he would be her only love, and she could not push him out of her mind or her heart.

'Frances, your trip abroad has been a success. You have improved,' remarked her mama. 'Although, I cannot think why this has happened — after living in a jungle as you were.'

Frances smiled.

Her mother chatted on, 'Yes, I think the way you arrange your hair now is most becoming. You look blooming, my dear — although do I detect you are a little sad?'

'Mama,' Frances interrupted her so that she was not forced to admit she was in love, 'I should like some new clothes.'

That suggestion pleased her mother immensely, who immediately began to relate what she knew about the newest fashions and shops in Bath and Bristol. 'My dear, you should see the attractive tiered skirts. And the bonnets trimmed with feathers, flowers and loops of ribbon.'

Before Frances had met George, she had not cared a jot about her clothes being in fashion. That was not true now as she was flattered by the admiring comments made about Maria's hair-style for her. And many of her clothes did need replacing after her long stay in Mexico, so she looked forward to seeing what materials were being sold in the draper's store and what fashion designs the dressmakers were using. Being tall for once did not bother her, as the newer styles, her mama told her, looked stylish on a slender, tall woman like Frances.

It was not until a day later, while unpacking her travelling bags, that Frances froze on hearing her maid shriek — and then continue screaming.

'Whatever is the matter?' her mother cried, almost dropping the fine china teacup she was holding.

Frances hoped fervently that the maid had not discovered one of the huge Mexican spiders hiding in her trunk. Running upstairs and hastening to the room where the maid had been taking Frances's clothes out of her trunk, piling up her folded petticoats to place in her chest of drawers, what Frances saw also made her heart beat faster and lift her hands in shock.

'My goodness!'

In the folds of her personal linen was a life-sized grotesque green face, fearsome with its staring eyes and gaping red mouth.

It was a magnificent green jade mask!

The maid had bolted, terrified, from the bedroom, while Frances looked at the Mayan Indian face with fascination. Was it not the ancient jade mask George wanted to conceal from the thieves? She was sure it was. And turning over more of her underclothes, she found a beautiful carved jade necklace, and a little lidded jade jar.

'My goodness!' Frances had to smile. She remembered telling George she had hidden Colonel Washburton's pistol in her underwear, and in haste, he had obviously decided it was the safest place to hide the Mexican treasures. So he must have asked Maria to put them in her luggage.

She carefully picked up the mask. It was a masterpiece of craftsmanship, awesome in its portrayal of a past Mexican king. Pieces of green jade had been cleverly fitted together to form the shape of the eyes, nose, mouth and ear lobes. The powerful, staring expression on the face reflected the superiority of the Mayan Indian's great early civilisation.

She stood admiring the objects until her mama rushed in. 'What on earth is the matter? Mary was sobbing so much, I was obliged to send her home.'

Frances immediately hid the jade mask under a pair of drawers, so as not to scare her mother, but showed her the ancient necklace. 'This is not my necklace, Mama. I must make sure it goes to the Mexican Embassy in London. Is it not lovely?'

Handling the jade with care, her mother agreed the carving was masterly. 'And the green jade is exquisite too,' she said. 'But what upset Mary?'

'I have also a mask with a face like a roaring tiger, Mama. Mary came across it, not expecting it, and it gave her a fright. That's all.'

'May I see the mask?'

'I think not, Mama, it may frighten you too.'

Her mother looked doubtful. 'Oh dear, I suppose I had better not look at it. I do not wish to suffer nightmares.'

Frances laughed. 'I shall show it to Papa because I am sure he would love to see it. Then I shall pack it up and make sure it gets back to Mexico safely. That is what George would want me to do.'

She gazed out of the window at the sky with its billowing white puffs of clouds, wondering if George was safe. 'George had to hide these ancient treasures from the men who were smuggling works of art out of Mexico — and so unknown to me he hid them in my trunk.'

Her mother sat down on her bedroom chair. 'I was wondering when you would mention George Webster,' she said. 'Gina told me about him.'

Shocked to learn that her love for George had been told to her mother by her aunt, Frances was embarrassed. But as they began to chat, Frances was glad to be able to confide in her mama and to tell her all about him, and her admiration for him. 'But I do not think he loves me,' she added sadly. 'We had little chance to discuss our feelings. There was always his work — '

'If George loves you, when he has finished his work over there, however long it takes, I am sure he will come to you,' Mrs Cannon said, as a woman who knew what love for a man meant.

Frances smiled with watering eyes at her mama.

'Yes,' continued her mother, 'love for a man can be painful, as well as glorious. But I think we must wait and see what the future has in store for you. In the meantime, do try not to frighten my maids!'

Frances laughed despite her tears, saying she did not think she had any more surprises in her luggage — without mentioning the possibility of exotic insects that might have crawled in her trunk.

So Frances did not mope. She had plenty to occupy her time: making beautiful flower drawings and shopping. Of course, she wrote immediately to the Mexican embassy in London to inform them that she had some Mayan objects she thought they should have — being careful to not to mention too much about what they were, or where they had come from. She did not want burglars coming to raid the house looking for them.

It was the first time Frances had really enjoyed accompanying her mother on her visits to Bath — an enjoyment for them both, because Caroline Cannon was now exceedingly proud of her daughter. Many compliments, instead of criticisms, were being made about Frances, who now expertly wound her golden mane up on her head and walked with the graceful saunter of South American women.

One day the Cannon household was surprised and honoured to receive a visit from a high-ranking Mexican official, the Plenipotentiary Minister, who was returning to Mexico because an Ambassador had just been appointed. The Minister had come to Bath to take charge of the precious jade objects Frances had discovered in her luggage.

His grand gilt decorated carriage brought the neighbourhood alive with gossip. But as Professor Arthur Cannon and his extraordinary daughter were well known for being individual, the visit was watched eagerly, but discreetly, by neighbours peeping through their windows. As far as the neighbours were concerned, it merely added to their gossip about the adventurous Cannon family. Being able to talk about the unusual Cannons over a cup of coffee in the Pump Rooms made their own humdrum lives a little more exciting.

On seeing the ancient jade treasure, the moustached, formally dressed minister was moved to tears, thanking Frances on behalf of his government and people for protecting the Mayan objects.

'It is Mr George Webster, not I, whom you have to thank for saving your treasures,' Frances explained. 'I hope you can tell me that he is well?'

'Indeed ma'am, he has now recovered after he was hurt in a fight — '

Frances put her hands over her mouth as she gasped loudly.

The official said quickly, 'Do not worry, ma'am. It is all over now, and we value the detective work Mr George Webster has done for us. He has been rewarded and decorated by General Santa Anna for his bravery.' He gave her a wide smile, and bowed formally — so that Frances felt like the young Queen Victoria. 'But you too deserve this medal, which I now present to you in gratitude for your part in protecting our Mayan treasures.'

Professor Cannon and wife looked at each other in astonishment as she was presented with a satin-lined box in which lay a gleaming golden medal.

Mrs Cannon exploded. 'Frances, you have not told us your part in this!'

Frances blushed. 'Mama, it is rather complicated to explain. I just happened to discover a historic site when I fell down a hole in the jungle.'

Her mother gasped.

'And later, I made some drawings of things that were found, which may have been useful. Then, after a few items were stolen, Mr Webster found them and I presume he put them in my luggage to keep them safe. But now they are rightfully going to be returned to Mexico.'

Frances didn't tell the Minister they been hidden in her undergarments!

She would have loved to be able to give the minister a message to take to George, to tell him that the green jade treasures were on the way back to Mexico. But neither he, nor she, had any idea where George was.

★ ★ ★

After that excitement, weeks went by and Frances worked at her flower paintings almost in a daze, thinking primarily of George. She enjoyed being taken by her mother to the Cathedral, the Assembly Rooms for afternoon tea, to the theatre on occasion, meeting polite society and discovering that Bath had some excellent shops.

Many a matron noticed in surprise that Miss Frances Cannon had acquired the sophisticated air of a married woman and wondered how an unmarried girl could have developed such poise in a jungle.

Frances smiled at their curious glances, thinking it was just as well they did not know she had briefly been Mrs George Webster!

One bright sunny morning, attired in a sprigged cream day dress with a fashionable basque jacket, Frances was walking back from the shops with some braid Mama had wanted when she spied a tall, well-dressed gentleman way ahead of her. His top hat made him appear even taller; he dwarfed most other men in sight. But it was his walk she recognised . . .

Her breathing became difficult. She could not chase after him. She could not call out to him — it would be unladylike in a place like Bath.

And what if she was mistaken, and the gentleman was not after all George Webster?

Frances's heart beat faster as the tall gentleman stopped walking to observe the terraced houses on his right, as if checking the house numbers. Then he stepped smartly up to her parents' front door and rang the bell.

'It is George!' she sobbed to herself, quickening her steps.

He was shown inside the house before Frances could hurry there. Panting, she stood on the pavement trying to stop trembling before letting herself in. Heart pounding, she took off her gloves and bonnet and handed them to the maid, who said, 'There's ever such a tall gentleman come asking to see you, Miss!'

Frances had difficulty keeping her voice steady. 'Thank you, Biddy,' she managed to say.

After the maid had gone, Frances checked her appearance in the hall mirror. She was so nervous that she did not notice how her complexion glowed after her walk, nor how well her new gown fitted her; nor how charming her hair was, swept up on her head in the manner Maria had taught her. She did see that she did not look serene, and appeared nervous.

Do not be an idiot, she told herself. *You wanted George to come, and so he has. Calm yourself. Go and meet him. And you can hold your head high because George will still be taller than you.*

Having used a pot pourri leaf to refresh her face and to pat her hands and wrists, Frances walked to the drawing room, hearing George's deep voice addressing her parents. 'Your daughter saved my life,' he was saying.

As Frances entered, the three were sitting in a cosy circle. George turned and got to his feet, smiling at her with delight as he bowed.

'And George saved my life, too, on one occasion,' Frances said — her nervousness almost gone, so she was able to smile too.

'No,' George corrected her, with a hint of teasing. 'I did not save you — it was that howler monkey.'

'A howler monkey?' Mrs Cannon exclaimed, horrified.

'Yes, ma'am,' affirmed George. 'A Mexican monkey that howls. Let me see if I can give you some idea of the most distinctive noise it makes — '

Seeing George about to demonstrate the monkey's blood-curdling cry, Frances said quickly, 'George, please, recollect how I told you Mama is very sensitive.' Moving closer, she whispered to him, 'She dislikes even creepy crawly things, like beetles and snakes — unless you want to make her faint.'

'Oh yes, I do remember now. I apologise, Frances.'

Their eyes met and they smiled. Frances longed for him to gather her into his arms and to kiss her, but he seemed a little uneasy.

Mama rose. 'Arthur, I do not think I want to hear about howling monkeys and other jungle animals. I want you to show me the new orchids which you told me are coming into flower. Come along.' She added in a low voice, 'I think the young people would prefer to discuss their adventures without us.'

Professor Cannon was only too keen to get back to his orchids. Offering his arm for his wife to take, they quietly left the room.

George looked unsure of what to say after her parents had left, so Frances enquired, 'Are you satisfied now that your work is finished?'

He grinned. 'I am, thank you.'

She looked deeply into his eyes. 'Did you catch the thieves?'

'Oh yes, we did.'

She sat down. 'Tell me all about it.'

He did not sit but strolled up and down the room. 'I would say I was far from clever, and got a beating from the rogues before they were captured. But I helped. Sam Stanley was able to catch the villainous organiser, Mr Clipperspite. Do you remember that little businessman on board ship with the shoe salesman? Both were in the illicit art trade in antiquities — shipping the Mayan treasures to be sold in London.'

Frances did. 'But they looked so *ordinary*. You would never think they had done any harm to anyone or anything.'

George gave a laugh. 'Indeed that was part of their disguise. But Sam Stanley was on to them long before I was. Clipperspite cleverly attached himself to me when he knew I was investigating the smuggling racket.'

'And did Sam Stanley not help you?'

'He did eventually, but I was trapped by Clipperspite and his men before I realised who the real villains were.'

Frances looked at him sympathetically. 'They might have killed you.'

George grimaced. 'I knew they would not kill me because they wanted the jade. And I refused to tell them where I had hidden it.'

'In amongst my small clothes!'

After a merry laugh, George said seriously, 'I was desperate to hide the treasure quickly, but also loath to involve you. My greatest fear was that you might be harmed.'

'Do you really care about me?'

'Of course I do!' he cried, looking somewhat uncomfortable.

Frances decided that the past was over and what she had to think of was the future — with George. And she must be brave and find out if he truly loved her. Moving close, she looked up at his beloved face. 'I care about you, too. And now the jade treasure is safely back with the Mexicans. So what is bothering you?'

'You, Mrs Webster.'

Frances gave a little laugh. 'Why should I cause you any more trouble?'

George frowned. 'When you left Mexico, and I could not travel back with you, I wondered if you had found the jade. Also I was worried, until they were caught, that some of the gang might harm you.'

'As it happened I did not find the jade until I unpacked my trunk here. In fact, my maid unpacked it — and the mask almost frightened her to death!'

George smiled grimly. 'The mask is intended to scare people.'

'As I expect you know, the jade is back in Mexico, or well on the way.'

'Yes, I was told and was pleased to hear that. My mission is complete — with thanks to you.'

'I did very little. It was your determination to put things right.'

George came close to her. 'Of course you helped me.'

Frances batted her eyelashes. 'How? I thought I had been nothing but a nuisance to you — so you told me.'

George laughed. 'I found a real treasure — you!' He put his hands gently on her arms, and looked deeply into her eyes, 'You helped me to overcome my fears.'

'Your fears? I thought you were quite at home in the jungle?'

'Frances, I am not talking about being in the jungle. I am talking about you setting a convict free.'

Frances looked up into his eyes,

puzzled. 'But — but I thought they had released you because they found you were not guilty.'

'That is so.' He gently clasped her close to his chest as he explained. 'The scars of my wrongful imprisonment remained with me — until I met you. I was able to talk to you, alone in our tent. And you listened patiently to my story and offered me hope for the future.'

Frances asked huskily, 'And what is your future going to be?'

'I was wondering . . . '

Frances held her breath.

George licked his lips. 'You may feel you should not accept a jailbird.'

Frances breathed out. 'You told me you were not the criminal, and that you were soon released.'

'That is true. But my imprisonment, although false, disgraced my family. Many people may still think I may have been guilty.'

Frances felt a surge of sorrow that such a brave, honest man could be haunted by a crime he did not commit

— and how cruelly judgmental people could be.

'But that is monstrous! I'm sure your family will be understanding about your misfortune. You must visit them and explain.'

'Yes, yes, I intend to. When I feel I have good reason to.'

Frances looked surprised. 'What reason are you looking for, for heaven's sake? Take the medal the Mexicans gave you, that will impress your worth upon them, surely.'

'I was thinking of taking more than a medal — a treasure I have found.'

They stood holding hands, looking searchingly at each other. She could smell his delectable shaving soap. His eyes seemed to possess the glittering beauty of green jade.

He cleared his throat with determination. 'So I came here today to ask you whether you would be willing to become Mrs Webster once again?'

Frances swallowed. Several things ran through her brain. Had he another exploration in mind? Another criminal case to investigate, or a thief to catch, where she might be useful?

'Dear me, George,' she said. 'Don't tell me you have been asked to chase another gang of criminals? I doubt if I can help, much as I'd like to.'

She felt him gently squeeze her. 'Frances, I cannot predict what might lie ahead for me. I only know that I want to pursue my life as a photographer, as an explorer — and most of all as a loving husband.'

All his worries had now been explained. His reticence was abandoned. His desire expressed. He was asking her to become Mrs Webster in reality — not pretending, as before.

Laughing gently she thought she would tease him. 'You mean you want me to share your snubs for being put in jail by mistake? You want me to help you to make peace with your family? Travel to the ends of the earth, and possibly suffer all kinds of hardships? And you want my help with your bulky

191

photographic equipment now you won't have Sam Stanley to do it? To say nothing of the dangers you might get yourself into, working for the police?'

George released her and reached for his hat. 'Hmm. That may be partly the truth of it.' Then he looked slightly apologetic. 'I am sorry, Miss Cannon. I believe I may have taken too much for granted.'

Frances took a deep breath and put her arms around his neck. 'George, I should love to become Mrs Webster again. I shall willingly visit your family with you, and help explain about the wrong that was done you, and inform them of what a wonderful man you really are. In fact, I would go anywhere in the world with you.'

'Frances, my love, thank you.'

When Mrs Cannon returned to the drawing room to ask Mr Webster if he cared to have luncheon with them, she hastily withdrew, seeing Mr Webster had his arms around her daughter, and had better things to do.

We do hope that you have enjoyed reading this large print book.

Did you know that all of our titles are available for purchase?

We publish a wide range of high quality large print books including:
Romances, Mysteries, Classics
General Fiction
Non Fiction and Westerns

Special interest titles available in large print are:
The Little Oxford Dictionary
Music Book, Song Book
Hymn Book, Service Book

Also available from us courtesy of Oxford University Press:
Young Readers' Dictionary
(large print edition)
Young Readers' Thesaurus
(large print edition)

For further information or a free brochure, please contact us at:
Ulverscroft Large Print Books Ltd.,
The Green, Bradgate Road, Anstey,
Leicester, LE7 7FU, England.
Tel: (00 44) 0116 236 4325
Fax: (00 44) 0116 234 0205

Other titles in the
Linford Romance Library:

CHERRY BLOSSOM

Patricia Keyson

Cherry's narrow boat home is sinking and she's persuaded to stay in a chalet at the hotel where she works. Cherry is smitten with the rather distant owner, Oliver. And despite his cool and aloof manner, she has never felt such passion, even towards her ex-husband. Oliver's brother, Darius, is far easier company. Whatever happens, she will always put the welfare of her son, Jay, first. Who will Cherry choose?